THE DRAGON'S FORBIDDEN OMEGA

THE DRAGON'S FORBIDDEN OMEGA

DARKVALE DRAGONS #3

CONNOR CROWE

AN MPREG PARANORMAL ROMANCE

Cover Art by Melody Simmons

CONTENTS

When the kids are away, the mates will play...

Sign up here for your FREE copy of ONE KNOTTY NIGHT, a special story that's too hot for Amazon!

https://dl.bookfunnel.com/c1d8qcu6h8

Facebook:

fb.me/connorcrowempreg

For my readers, who made this dream a reality

1

TORK

"You'd sooner find me with a bag over my head," I told Lucien with a scowl. "I'm not going to the ball, and I'm definitely not dressing up or wearing a mask."

Lucien's shoulders slumped. "Not even if I lend you one? It's been a long time since we had reason to celebrate, Tork. Join us. You don't have to dance or anything, but there's going to be a lot of food there, at the very least..."

There was no winning with this guy. He had a point, though. The last days, months, hell, years had been spent in isolation, battle, and a constant state of moving, running, protecting. Not to mention my buddy Marlowe just reunited with his long time love Nik and they had a darling baby girl. The smell of love was in the air, I guessed. Not too long ago Lucien himself had brought home a human mate, of all things.

There was so much to be grateful for.

When I looked at it that way, the Flower Festival was the most normal thing to happen to us in years. The Firefang tradition celebrated family, beauty, and each other. It had been a wonderful festival, and the week wound to a close with an extravagant ball complete with musicians, food from across the world, and jaw-dropping performances.

I huffed out a breath through my nose.

"Fine, I'll go." I held out my hand. "But I'm gonna need that mask."

My lips quirked up in a grin, and Lucien's did the same. "I knew I'd get you to see reason." He shook my hand briskly, then his eyes glinted again.

That meant there was a "but..." coming.

"Now there's the matter of your date."

I rolled my eyes. "Don't push your luck. We gonna go get that mask or stand around talking?"

Lucien led the way off toward his home but kept talking. "We're not on the battlefield anymore, Tork. I bet there's more than one omega out there that would love to have you."

"It's not like that," I shrugged. "I've got everything I need already. Date...mate...it's all the same. All a distraction, if you ask me."

Lucien chuckled. "Whatever you say."

I grumbled and quickened my steps to keep up with him. "Let's just get this over with."

We arrived at the door to Lucien's home and he swiveled to face me before opening the door.

"A tip from your Clan Alpha? Keep your eyes open. Never know what you might find."

————

The bubbly champagne burst across my tongue and tingled as it went down. I sat down the glass flute and gazed out at the couples gliding across the floor in merriment.

Alphas and omegas of all shapes and sizes had come out to the ball tonight, humans and shifters alike. I scratched my chin underneath the full-face mask Lucien had lent me. At least no one would recognize me like this.

The clash of floral scents hung heavy in the air, making me a little lightheaded, if I was being honest. Perhaps that was just the drink, though. Lucien twirled around on the dance floor with his mate in his arms, both of them wearing expressions of unfettered joy. They clung to one another so closely, as if they were one person instead of two.

Must be nice.

I couldn't help thinking about what Lucien had said on the way to pick up my costume. Sure, I was busy with work and loved what I did, but that didn't change the fact that I was a dragon shifter, and an alpha at that. My beast, much as I didn't like to admit it, had needs too.

Needs that I'd been willfully ignoring more often than not. I told myself I didn't need anyone, that it would be too complicated, too messy. I'd seen plenty of relationships go sour, including my parents'. I wasn't in a hurry to replicate that any time soon.

But the way people like Lucien and Alec looked at one another was different. Any bystander could clearly see they adored one another, trusted one another, leaned on one another when the other couldn't be strong. Maybe it wouldn't be so bad to have someone like that.

Keep your eyes open, Lucien had warned me. I straightened my back, squared my shoulders, and ran a hand through my hair to slick the wavy strands back across my forehead.

A dangerous scheme began to brew in my head as my dragon twisted its way through my chest, aching for release. I hadn't lain with anyone in a long, long time. Longer than even I could remember.

Don't you want something like that? My dragon urged me on. I glanced at the couples again.

Yes. Yes I did.

What if I could learn to let go, just for a night? What kind of man could keep up with not only my fast-paced lifestyle but the dangerous nature of my profession?

Not many, that was for sure.

I raked my gaze over the crowd. There were plenty of single omegas in dashing costumes, but none of them caught my eye. Lace and flowers and dyes assaulted my eyeballs at every turn, and they were lovely, yes, but who could say what kind of man lie beneath?

Fuck it, I shrugged. *One night is hardly forever.*

My stomach growled in protest after the multiple rounds of champagne and no food. "Fine," I muttered to myself and pushed through the crowd to the snack bar.

A delicious array of fruits, cheeses, crackers, and other delicacies decorated the long serving table, all arranged in artful patterns while the ball-goers filled plates and chatted among themselves.

I had my eye on a chocolate-covered strawberry when

my hand brushed a silk glove reaching for the same morsel. I jerked my wrist away, looking up in surprise.

A thin, shorter man stood before me, decked out in an elaborate costume of black, cream, and gold. He cut quite the dashing figure; even under the intricate swirls of the mask he wore I could see glowing embers of eyes.

A spark shot up my arm as we touched. Even through the silk glove, his presence was electrifying. I could tell right away that he was an omega, but his floral perfume covered any other scent coming off him.

"Excuse me," the man said softly and drew his hand back, shoving it behind his back.

The strawberry, chocolate covered or not, was all but forgotten. My gaze rested on the flamboyant omega, so different from the shifters I was used to seeing. Perhaps it was something in the man's voice. Something in the way he held himself or the way he slightly tilted his head when considering me. Whatever it was, I couldn't shake the feeling I knew him from somewhere.

I shook my head. Maybe I'd had a few too many glasses of that champagne. I fought back the urge to say "do I know you?" and instead offered a greeting. "Good evening."

"Is it?" The man asked quizzically, now leaning over me to fill his plate. A smell wafted off of him I'd never noticed before. It was omega, all right, but different

6

than the other shifters I'd been in contact with in the village. There was only the faintest hint of it, but as I considered the omega smell grew stronger, and stronger still.

My mind reeled and I yanked my gaze away as he straightened with his plate.

He cocked an eyebrow in my direction.

"It's the Flower Festival," I said, suddenly flustered. "The ball. Most people wait all year for such an occasion." And surely this one's costume was long in the making. The sequins caught my eye in the light, feathers blossomed from his shoulders, and he presented himself with all the elegance of a jeweled peacock.

The omega shrugged. "I'm not most people."

That was for certain.

I gave an amused chuckle as that current of desire flickered through my veins again. "Nor am I, Sparkles." I grinned at the nickname, stroking my chin. Where did I know him from? Surely somewhere, right? I would have noticed such an omega before.

Now he'd roused me both body and mind. I wanted, no, needed to know more about him. But not here.

Sparkles tilted his head away from the snack bar to a quieter corner of the ballroom, shrouded by heavy velvet drapes and whispering couples. He pointed at his ear and gestured for me to come close.

I held my breath as I leaned in. The scent of him poured off his skin and invaded my senses, lighting up my dragon from deep within.

He'd do. He'd do nicely, the dragon crooned.

"It's a bit loud around here, yes? I'd like to hear the man I'm talking to."

I nodded and Sparkles led the way. He slipped through gaps in the crowd so easily, twisting and turning as he danced to the rhythm of the music. I...well, let's just say I wasn't nearly so graceful. After a few awkward jostles and mumbled apologies, I made it to the other side of the room. Only, Sparkles was nowhere to be found.

"Over here!" His glittery head poked out from behind a large flowerpot and waved at me. He patted a plush cushion in an alcove where tiny globes of dragonfire floated on garlands and gave off a flickery, cozy light. Totally romantic...if I was into that kind of thing.

I grabbed another glass of champagne from a passing server and joined him, my long legs sticking off to the side of the planter. *Not so private now*, I chuckled to myself.

Sparkles continued to eye me. Was he struggling with

the same hidden mystery I was? Was he feeling the same inklings of desire?

I took another sip to steel myself and leaned back against the cushions. My ears rang. I hadn't realized just how loud the ball was with all the people and music and talking. But now that I was away from it all, my senses were still catching up.

Delicate hands picked up a strawberry and popped it into his mouth. I couldn't help but watch the way those luscious lips closed around the fruit. Couldn't help but wonder what they might feel like around my...

"I'm not much for crowds," Sparkles said sheepishly, interrupting my wayward thoughts.

"I never would have guessed," I teased. He carried himself like a peacock, but perhaps it was all an act? A character he put on like a costume for this occasion alone?

A hint of chocolate smeared on the corner of his mouth. A vision flashed through my mind of grabbing him right then and there, of licking that sweet filling off and so much more. This was so unlike me. I shook my head and put a hand to my temple.

Other alphas got all worked up over sex and mating.

Not me.

I swallowed hard, straightening and taking a deep

breath. Wrong choice. I got a lungful of that intoxicating scent and my cock grew even harder as I watched him enjoy the strawberries one at a time. He closed his eyes as he bit into each one, a low sigh escaping from his lips.

"You really like strawberries," I chuckled, grasping for what to say next.

"They're my favorite," Sparkles agreed. "And the chocolate...mmm! I haven't had chocolate in years. Such a delicacy! This has been the best Flower Festival ever, wouldn't you say?"

His eyes locked with mine and I couldn't tear myself away. I was trapped there, held in this omega's burning gaze as he set the plate aside. The familiar rumbling of fire rose in my chest, sparked on my tongue. But this time it was more than a passing annoyance. It was a strong, all-encompassing heat that soaked through me and wiped out all other thoughts.

Take him, my dragon screeched. *Take him now!*

I couldn't taste the champagne on my lips. Couldn't smell the fresh scent of the flowers. There was only him. I drew closer to him as if pulled by some external force, my lips slightly parted as I honed in on that perfect mouth...

"Oh, shit!" Sparkles yelped in what sounded like pain and shrunk away from me. I blinked, my mind screeching to a halt with the whiplash. The omega scrambled to his feet and put a hand to his forehead, wringing his hands. "Shit, shit, shit!"

"What?" I rasped, my voice husky. Lust still simmered there, hot and ready, but there was something else, too. My protective alpha instincts kicked into full gear. What was wrong? Had I hurt him?

"I'm...oh, Goddess, I'm so sorry, I have to..."

Sparkles scrambled off through the crowd without another word, disappearing easily among the throng.

"Wait!" I called after him, lumbering to my feet and scanning the crowd. He might have been small, but I could see over many of the bobbing heads. Not to mention that costume made him pretty easy to find.

There he was.

I pushed through dancers and servers, accidentally trampling a few toes on the way. I knocked over a wobbly vase and it shattered on the ground in an explosion of glass. It only barely registered in my mind as I fled toward him, every alpha instinct roaring to the surface. My heart leapt into double time as my eyes locked on to his small form, crouched and panting near the end of a long hallway. His eyes widened in fear when he saw me.

Not so sparkly anymore.

That's when I realized what was happening. Why his smell had come on so strong. An unexpected heat, right in the middle of the whole town.

Goddess, no wonder he was panicked.

I held up my hands in a gesture of peace, taking a few cautious steps in his directions.

"Hey, it's okay. I'm here to help."

As much as my dragon wanted to take this omega right here right now, I pushed through it to a higher plane of reason. He needed help. He needed to get to safety before some less scrupulous alpha got to him first.

The scent and energy in the air was electric. It crackled with power and arousal and possibility. And I couldn't have any of it.

Sparkles shrank back further, his small body quivering.

"I'm not going to hurt you," I said slowly, and our eyes locked.

There. Hidden within those masked depths was the shining amber core I was looking for. It called to me like a magnet to my soul.

Mate...? The word bounced around in my soul but I pushed it away. It couldn't be. Not here. Not now.

I took a breath and extended my hand. "Let me help you."

"You know what this is, don't you?" The omega whispered, voice shaking. His forehead shone with sweat and the very visible evidence of his arousal pressed through his pleated pants.

"Yes," I growled.

Focus, Tork, focus.

I grit my teeth and reached out to him, knowing what I'd feel when our skin touched. But I couldn't leave him here. That wouldn't be honorable at all.

"Should I be scared?" He breathed.

"No," I assured him, and he took my hand.

His skin on mine lit up every pore, every nerve, every cell. My vision narrowed to focus on him, only him. "I won't hurt you," I assured him and gave the hand a squeeze. "There are other alphas I would not be so sure about, but you're in good hands. You're safe with me. Let's get you out of here."

I looked to my left and right down the hallway. No one was coming, which was good. No one to see our particular predicament. I ducked around a corner and found a spare room. "Come on," I beckoned. Sparkles followed.

The omega sank down onto a plush couch as I slid the door closed. It wasn't exactly the lap of luxury, but we could hide out here until the crowds died down, then make our escape. Sparkles let out a sigh and put a hand to his head, swaying a bit before righting himself.

"Do you need water? A blanket? Anything I can get you?" The words tumbled out on top of one another. Speaking too fast again. I wanted, no, needed to help him, and seeing the look on his face made me even more concerned. My pulse raced in my veins and my dragon begged for release as I realized just how close we were.

We were alone. Alpha and omega. And he was in heat.

Goddess help me.

I wanted him more than I'd ever wanted anything. More than the new chemicals for my lab. More than a new adventure. This little omega *was* the adventure, and this was an adrenaline rush greater than the most action-packed heist. Red flags flew up in all directions in the back of my mind, but the intoxicating smell of an omega in heat wiped them all away.

I promised to look after him, and I had to do that. No matter how much my cock ached.

"I'll just be outside, I'll watch the door and send for someone to help..." I needed air. Yes, that was it.

My hand was on the doorknob when the omega responded.

"No," he rasped. "Stay."

I turned slowly to face him, blood roaring in my ears and sparks crackling on my tongue. Did he know what he was doing to me?

"Are you sure about that?" I rumbled, my self restraint holding on by only a thread. "In your condition..."

He leapt to his feet and grabbed my hands, pressing me into the door. His scent smothered me. I was lost. The omega's lips whispered over my chest, my neck. He looked up, locking eyes with mine.

"I said...stay."

Even through our masks I could see the flaming desire there, like molten metal ready to be forged. My body strained against him as he pressed me against the wall, and even though I could easily push him away, I didn't want to.

May I be damned, but I didn't want to.

"You wanted to help me. So help me," he whispered. His hand was soft in mine, only a few callouses on the fingers and palm. I didn't care. He led my hand to his bulging crotch and left it there. My eyes widened and I sucked in a breath. Omegas were known to be forward while in heat, but this was something else.

"I can't," I groaned through gritted teeth. I'd never lost control like this before. Never. I prided myself on it.

But here I was, every inhibition and shred of decency gone. It should have been humiliating.

But I'd never been so turned on in my life.

"Please," the omega moaned. He fumbled with the layers of costume and soon the bottoms came free, exposing his hard and leaking cock.

The moment I saw it, there was no turning back. My dragon roared to the surface, blocking all out reason, all honor. This omega was mine.

2

TORK

"You sure about this?" I rumbled, running a hand down the omega's cheek to his shoulders as I held him to me. Goddess, he was so warm. And he smelled incredible. Like my favorite food and my favorite hobbies all rolled into one.

This was my mate. Had to be. And to think I'd met him at the Flower Festival ball I'd been so reluctant to attend.

I smirked at the thought, remembering how Marlowe and Nik had first found one another at the Festival all those years ago.

Guess love was in the air.

"I want this," the omega mumbled. "Want you."

That was enough for me.

My alpha senses took over as I loomed over the small omega. He was small, yes, but with a fire that roused me even further. What was it about this man that stood out among all the others? Whatever it was, I was going to find out.

Right after I buried my cock all the way to the hilt in his sweet, hot channel. Right after I made him mine.

"Is here okay?" I asked, arranging a pile of pillows and laying him down gently. It took all my resolve to keep from throwing him down and taking what was mine, but I was better than my instincts. Omegas deserved to be loved and treasured, not fucked and discarded like pieces of meat.

I was going to treasure this one with all I had.

"Take off your mask," he breathed, eyes shining. "Want to see you."

I froze at that. Peeling away the layers of mask and costume might break the spell between us. I recognized it as an irrational fear, but couldn't bat it away for long before it resurfaced.

"We have our whole lives to look upon one another," I replied, toying with the feathers that splayed out around his head like a crown. "Tonight, let's preserve the magic."

My omega was silent for a moment, still holding my gaze, our dragons reaching out to one another in a primal dance neither of us could resist. Now or never.

"Fair enough," he responded, and kissed me.

It took a moment to get over the initial shock. Not only was this omega the hottest shifter I'd ever seen, but he was willing to take the initiative, too. My dragon growled in response and I pressed myself closer, spearing my tongue into his mouth as he opened to me with a moan. We clasped at one another, giving and taking that delicious chemistry that flowed between us.

This wasn't just the champagne. This wasn't just a fling.

This was fate, and both our dragons knew it.

It didn't matter that I didn't even know his name. It didn't matter that I couldn't shake the strange feeling of familiarity. All that mattered was getting inside him, joining us the way we were meant to be joined, as alpha and omega.

I wasted no time in fumbling with the buttons on the tunic Lucien had lent me. My fingers rushed over the brass fast and clumsy. I feared I'd rip away a button or tear right through the fabric for a harrowing moment, and then the fasteners came free. My mate sucked in a breath at the sight of my bare chest, toned and muscled from long days of working in the shop. Demolitions and magitech was no easy business, and I had to be on my toes, both physically and mentally, to do the work I did.

One false move could mean death, after all.

Sparkles followed suit, divesting himself of the glittery garment and tossing it aside. It crumpled to the floor, forgotten, and I grabbed him with such ferocity he squeaked in surprise. The feeling of skin on skin burned me up from the inside out. Already I could feel the pull of his dragon to mine. Already I could feel the ancient mating rite beginning as our souls reached out and intertwined.

"Fuck," the omega breathed, and I leaned down to plant kisses across his smooth, toned chest, his sides, down to his abdomen. He sucked in a breath and I continued my trail of pleasure, nipping at his hips, his thighs, and finally centering in on his hard and weeping cock.

"You're beautiful," I rumbled, admiring his proud length.

"What are you gonna do about it?" He quirked an eyebrow.

Goddess, I could get used to this.

I slipped a hand out from around his back to snake down toward his crotch, watching the contortions of my mate's face as I went. Even behind the mask, I could see the gasps and moans of pleasure perfectly. And I hadn't even touched his cock yet. I shuddered to think of what came next.

When I reached his opening, my fingers came away soaking wet. I brought them up to my face and sniffed, the pheromones surrounding me and blocking out everything else. With a throaty groan, I slipped a slick finger into my mouth. Flavors exploded on my tongue, musk and herbs and the overwhelming feeling that this was *right*.

My mate looked up at me with wide eyes. He wiggled his hips toward me, mewling with desire as his cock twitched. I wasted no time getting rid of my pants and my cock sprung free, hot and heavy against my already overheated skin. I propped myself on one arm and leaned over him, gathering our cocks together in one hand.

The omega hissed. "Goddess..." he swore.

"More where that came from." Sparks of need zigzagged all over my body as I pressed our cocks together. The friction built and my balls tightened. I would come right here if I wasn't careful. The omega's velvety length slid easily against mine, making my dragon all kinds of crazy.

"Please," the omega panted. "Now." He lifted his hips

and angled himself toward me. My heart nearly stopped—I'd never seen anything so hot in my life.

My human mind went blank, but that didn't matter. The dragon took full control and I guided my cock where it needed to go. My vision sharpened. Prisms of light danced before my eyes. This was it.

Gently at first, I hissed as his hot, tight channel enveloped my cock. I pressed into him inch by torturous inch and my heart sped into double time. As soon as I seated myself all the way to the hilt inside him, I let out a long, shuddery breath. This was what I was made for, what I'd been waiting for all these years. The old ideas about not needing a mate or not understanding the appeal faded into the background. This was better than flying.

My partner's arms wrapped around me and pulled me closer until I covered him with every inch of my skin. Only our faces remained concealed, but it added to the eroticism of the moment, if anything. I felt wild and free, burying myself in a mystery omega I never knew I needed. This was what people wrote songs about, I realized. This was what people went to war over.

The omega rocked beneath me, his breaths quickening as he dragged his small hands down my back. I growled deep in my chest and thrust into him again. My head still spun with the overwhelming sensations of his tight heat around me and the connection of our dragons, our souls. I let it spin. Wouldn't give this up for anything.

My dragon rose dangerously close to the surface and I tasted fire, felt my fingers morph into claws as I pounded into my mate's wanting flesh. I fought to keep from shifting on the spot. Shifting indoors would bring down a whole pile of rubble on top of us.

Decidedly not sexy.

The omega beneath me seemed to be struggling as much as I was as his eyes and reptilian pupils flickered between human and dragon form. He was getting close, I realized as he squeezed me with his legs. This was the point of no return.

Mine! My dragon soared within me, and I pushed into him one, two, three more times. Then the world shattered around us. I let out a roar as my knot swelled, locking us together as mates. I'd never felt so full, so wanted in all my years. And with the spirits looking down on us from above, I shuddered and filled the omega with my seed, panting, as we held on to each other for dear life.

Mine. My mate. My destiny.

———

It wasn't supposed to end like this.

"*You've got to take care of Ansel. Please,*" *the weak words of a dying man rung in my ears. I held his limp body in my arms as fire and screams echoed around us. My best friend. My partner in crime.*

"*Don't say that.*" *I growled.* "*You're going to be okay.*" *I pressed a makeshift bandage into the wound at his side. It soaked through almost instantly. He was losing too much blood, and his eyes already had that glassy, far away stare.*

He was going to die.

Veltar gripped at my shirt with surprising strength for a dying man. "*Please, take care of my son. He will come of age soon, and he needs a mentor. I can think of no one better.*" *He coughed and his body shook. Blood bubbled on his lips.*

My entire body felt cold. Battle raged around me, but it was faint in my ears. My own aches and wounds meant nothing. In this moment, there was only us. As a warrior and a Firefang, I knew that death was part of life. But I never thought it would be like this. Without Veltar, who was I? What was I? I was an alpha, and a weapons scientist. I had no idea how to take care of a child.

My throat dried as I watched my Veltar's life force fade before my eyes. There was nothing I could do.

"*Please...*" *Veltar panted.* "*Promise me, Tork.*"

"I promise," I swore, and Veltar passed into the Great Beyond.

———

That dream again.

My heart ached and a lump of emotion still wobbled in my throat, even nearly a decade after the fact. I groaned and opened my eyes to the shimmery rays of sunlight.

My body ached all over, and I had a raging headache. I was naked, which wasn't unusual, but the room was unfamiliar. What had happened last night?

Memories filtered back in slowly as the dream lost its hold on me. I sat up so fast I nearly fainted, my head protesting as I put a hand to my temple. The Flower Festival. The ball. The omega...

Oh, no. I didn't...

I snaked a hand down to my crotch. My cock was still sensitive from the night before, and my muscles screamed as if from the hardest workout. I could just about hear the grinding of gears in my brain as it rushed to process the new information.

Last night was the Flower Festival ball. Last night I ran across an inexplicably endearing omega. Last night I mated him.

So where was he?

The room was empty, save for a few pillows and a lingering floral smell. Guess I'd spooked the guy.

I scrubbed a hand across my face. What the hell had gotten into me? As one of Lucien's right hand men and head of weapons and demolition for the Firefangs, I needed to be calm and in control at all times.

And what happened last night? That was about as far from control as you could get.

As I quickly threw on my clothes and schooled my hair into some semblance of order, I pushed away the nagging anxiety that bubbled up in my gut.

My omega was out there. And I didn't even know his name.

W hat a night.

As soon as I woke up and found myself in a strange alpha's arms, I bolted. Didn't know what else to do.

Goddess-damned heat.

There I was, just trying to have a little fun at the Flower Festival ball. I'd made an outfit just for the occasion. It was one of the only times per year I got to have a little fun and dress up. Couldn't exactly go into work covered in feathers. *What a fire hazard that would be*, I chuckled to myself as I swung my legs over the side of the bed.

And then I'd went and done it. I slept with an alpha last night when my heat overtook me. Not only did we have sex, if my hazy memory was correct, he'd knotted in me too. That probably meant we were mated now, and probably meant I was gonna be carrying a little dragon inside me soon.

Conflicting thoughts and desires fought their way through my mind. Did I regret it? Not exactly, but the guilt was still there.

What would Tork say?

Ever since returning from a four year stint at Magitech Academy, I saw things in a new way. Returning to Darkvale after studying abroad had not only sharpened my skills as an engineer, but also my perceptions. I saw things, and people, in a new light. My mentor Tork, in particular.

He was handsome, no one could deny that. But he was also my father's best friend, and totally off limits.

I swallowed and buttoned up my flame-resistant tunic, stopping to glance in the mirror and make sure it was on straight. Couldn't tell you how many times I'd missed a button and came into work with a lopsided shirt.

After my parents passed away in battle when I was only thirteen, Tork took me in. I knew him from my childhood as my father's best friend, but in the year before I went off to the academy, he took care of me best he could and taught me what he knew.

I'd always had an inclination for engineering, sure, but getting to work alongside Tork? It was like a dream come true. He was incredibly brilliant, if a little brash, and I respected that about him. His rigorous training paid off once I got into Magitech Academy, and then I was off to learn amongst the greatest engineers in the country.

Now that I was back, I couldn't shake the feeling that there was something...I don't know, more for me out there. Getting back into my old routine of working in the lab and joining up with the local magitech guild was all fine and good, but my dragon, my omega, needed more.

I squeezed my eyes shut and drew in a long breath through my nose.

It wasn't like I was ever going to mate with Tork anyway. He was not only my mentor, but had served as a kind of father figure to me after my parents died. Talk about forbidden.

Brushing away the pangs of guilt, I threw on my jacket, slipped on my boots, and made my way out the door. Whatever had happened, I could deal with it later. For now, I had work to do.

———

"Yowch!" I hopped on one foot, holding my throbbing

toe after dropping a wrench on it for the second time that day. One of the other engineers eyed me warily, flipping up his welding mask to watch my theatrics.

"You doing all right there?" He asked, raising an eyebrow. "Forget your steel toe boots today?"

"It's nothing," I muttered. "Just clumsy today, is all." I put my throbbing foot back on the ground and tried to shoot him a smile.

"You're normally not like this," He pressed on, putting down his tools to approach me. "Why don't you take an early lunch break, clear your head?"

I swallowed and turned my head, staring at the ground. Now I was fucking things up at work too.

"We've got a lot of work to do and need everyone in top form. If there's anything I can do..."

"There's not," I cut him off, and grabbed my lunch sack. "I'll be fine."

I breezed out the door, my skin cooling rapidly in the breeze. I always worked up a sweat in the workshop. Who wouldn't? The place was covered with forges and fire. But out here, everything was quiet. I could finally hear myself think.

Putting a few paces between me and the workshop, I wandered over to a small clearing with a bench and a few trees. I thought better of it when I realized how popular as a lunch spot it would be. I didn't want to run into anyone right about now. Definitely not Tork.

I turned on my heel and headed off in the opposite direction, trying to ignore the unknown feeling of guilt that rose within me.

Why did I care so much about letting Tork down? He was my mentor, not my mate. There was nothing between us. I respected him in a totally business way, but that was it. That was all it would ever be.

I sunk down onto a fallen tree branch behind a building with a sigh. No one to bother me here.

The air hung silent save for the distant mechanical whirring and clanging of the workshop. Birds fluttered through the trees and the air carried the last fading scents of the Flower Festival. As enjoyable as it all was, reality started to filter back into day to day life here in Darkvale. Although things on the war front were calmer than they had been, there was still the matter of the mysterious "metal men" uncovered by our resident Sorcerer, Elias. I shivered at the thought as I took a bite of my sandwich. Lucien had recruited just about all of us engineers to research the possibility of this kind of contraption and to see if we could replicate something similar. We needed to know what we were up against, and if a raging automaton struck Darkvale now, we'd be woefully unprepared.

The sound of a snapping twig yanked me out of my thoughts and I looked up to find the man I least wanted to see right now.

Tork.

My cheeks flushed as I stared at him with a bit of bread hanging from my mouth. He stood there, hands on his hips. He panted as if he'd run all the way here. "There you are."

I put down the sandwich as a thread of fear twisted through me. Something was wrong. I didn't know what, but I could feel it, all the way down in my gut.

"What's the matter?"

"It's Lucien. He's got news of the metal men. Needs to meet with us immediately. All hands."

I nearly choked on my sandwich and swallowed hard. "He never calls unplanned all hands meetings."

"He does now. Come on." Tork outstretched his hand to help me up and I grabbed it without thinking.

A spike of electricity shot through me as we touched and I gasped before I could stop myself. I looked to Tork to see if he was feeling the same, but if he was, he didn't show it. Didn't expect him to—years of working together taught me he didn't exactly wear his heart on his sleeve.

Get your head in the game, I scolded myself, and yanked my hand away. I wiped it on my pants and slung my bag over my shoulder. "Let's go," I said, and we rushed off toward the workshop.

This was no time for worrying about mates and babies. I had a job to do. Grateful for the distraction, I pushed my legs harder, focusing on the wind in my hair and the cool breeze on my face. My clan needed us, and I wasn't about to let them down.

The mystery of my midnight mate would just have to wait.

————

"Come in, come in," Lucien ushered us through the door as he shut the heavy iron behind us with a eerily final thunk. "Thank you for coming on such short notice. I apologize for interrupting your lunch break," he lowered his eyes to me, "but I have urgent news from the field. And I need your help."

I hastily took my seat next to Tork and watched as Lucien walked over to the head of the crowd that had formed. My heart still raced and my blood felt like it was on fire. I told myself it was just the adrenaline of having a good run back to the shop and wondering what Lucien had to tell us, but with Tork sitting there so close to me, I couldn't be sure.

All of those worries seemed insignificant, though, as I listened to Clan Alpha Lucien's announcement.

"It is with a heavy heart that I bring you news from the field. We've received reports of these...metal men being sighted only a day's ride from here."

Murmurs of surprise and shock filled the crowd and my veins turned to ice as I considered the ramifications. All we had found were remnants...they found one operational?!

Lucien held up his hand for silence and I held my breath, waiting for the next bombshell to drop. "Yes, it does appear that our enemies have an early prototype afield, and in a skirmish we've lost not one, but two of our prized scouts." He placed a hand over his heart and looked upon us with sad eyes. "They are with the Goddess now, watching over us from the Great Beyond. But we shall not let this slight go unanswered. We must root out this prototype before it ever reaches our walls. The future of Darkvale, and of the Firefangs, depends on it. I've chosen several warriors and scouts to intercept and neutralize the threat, but I need engineers, as well. The road ahead will be dangerous, and I will not force you to fight. But think of this: your families, your children, your mates, all depend on what happens in the next few weeks. Will you join us?"

The room filled with muttering for a moment, each of us waiting for someone to speak up first.

"I will," I heard myself say. I stood, the wooden chair squealing behind me as I pressed my hands down on the table. "I will go with you." I needed a distraction. I needed time to think. And the chance to get up close and personal with such an elaborate specimen was just the icing on the cake.

"I'm coming too," Tork chimed in beside me almost instantly. He stood and gave me a glance I couldn't decipher. I tensed. So much for that idea.

Lucien nodded at us both and marked our names on a list. "We need one more."

"And I," Rex agreed with a dip of his head.

"It's decided," Lucien regarded us with a flick of his pen. "Glendaria smiles upon you. All others, you may leave. Tork, Ansel, and Rex, you'll need to attend the briefing. At dawn, we depart."

My stomach roiled at the thought as men and women pressed their way past us out of the workshop. The walls seemed to close in on me, and the air was suddenly too thick, too full with the pungent odors of oil and metal. I swallowed and tasted bile.

Spending who knew how long in close quarters with Tork was just about the last thing I wanted to do right now. He'd smell the alpha on me if he hadn't already, and if I was pregnant...

35

What would he think of me then?

Goddess help me, I prayed I wasn't making the wrong choice. I could barely stomach the idea of keeping this secret from him, especially when he'd find out soon enough. I had to clear the air before we left. It would be just too awkward otherwise.

I turned, hoping to find him still standing there next to me. "Tork, I wanted to—" The words were no sooner out of my mouth than the alpha slipped away through the doors, leaving the thoughts trapped on my tongue.

TORK

Dawn came much too early for my liking. I yawned and stretched, rolling over in bed and burying my face in the pillows for just a few more seconds.

I'd been in a lot of messy situations, but I'd never felt so dirty. Not even an hour-long shower with Myrony's best scrubbing gel could get rid of the thoughts that plagued my every waking moment.

Dishonor.

Shame.

Impropriety.

I was guilty of all three of those and so much more.

When I agreed to take Veltar's son under my wing, he became the number one priority in my life. Work and loyalty to the clan came a close second. With both of those duties taking up my time, there was no room for a mating.

And yet that was precisely what I'd done at the Flower Festival ball.

It was no wonder the omega hadn't sought me out after that scandalous night. Omegas went into heat at intervals, that much was known, but they usually kept to their homes when it occurred. Being caught out in public was a predicament indeed. I'd only wanted to protect him, care for him, keep him away from alphas that may do him harm.

And I became the very alpha I wanted to save him from.

He'd begged me for it in the heat of the moment, but didn't all omegas? I rubbed a hand over my face and threw myself out of bed as my front door rattled on the hinges.

"Coming!" I growled, gathering up my bag and slinging my sword over my shoulder. The door shook again, this time louder.

"The clan's gonna leave without you if you don't get your ass out here!"

"Goddess, give me a moment," I grumbled. I stashed a

few of my best reagents in a hip pouch and strapped my water flask to my side.

When I opened the door I found Arthur standing there, looking rather displeased.

"Bout time you showed up," he huffed. "Now come on, the rest of the group's already started moving!"

I picked up my steps and followed Arthur until we came to the giant gate at heading out of the city walls. Marlowe and Kari were there, along with Rex, another scout I couldn't name, and Ansel. I winced at the sight. I was gonna have to tell him sooner or later, but personal drama had no place during a military mission. We'd already lost two of our best scouts to the infernal contraption and if I didn't keep my wits about me, we'd lose even more.

"There you are," Marlowe nudged me as I joined their ranks heading out of the city. "Thought you weren't gonna make it."

"Slept in," I grumbled.

"As always," Kari said under her breath. I shot her a glare and she shut up.

"All right, Firefangs. Our mission is clear. Track down the prototype. Find out who's controlling it. Neutralize the threat. Engineers, you're to salvage everything you can and bring it back for dismantlement. Warriors:

you'll hold the line while the engineers do their work. Scouts: you'll clear the way and update our trackers. Is everyone ready?"

"Sir," we said in unison, and I felt the familiar splash of adrenaline.

This was going to be an adventure.

———

The journey started out well enough—all of us were in high spirits and we joked and chatted before getting too far beyond the walls. There would come a time for silence, and soon. Our good humor wore off quickly when the skies parted and unleashed a heavy rain on our heads. It slowed our progress and made the road like quicksand to walk through. We weren't talking and laughing anymore, no. More like the grumbles and grunts of exertion, and the slurping sound our boots made in the mud.

I avoided catching Ansel's eye. Didn't want to have to break the uncomfortable news to him while we were out in the field. Didn't want to break the news to him at all, really. But I'd have to sooner or later.

I had to admit I snuck a few glances in as he stumbled in the mud. The strangest pull came from deep in my gut, urging me forward to help him up. I didn't think much of it; I'd spent most of the last decade looking after him and mentoring him in the magitechnical arts, after all.

But that's not all, my dragon urged me on with a flicker of what almost felt like arousal. I shook my head and hoped the thoughts would leave. They didn't, only rolling about like the ball bearings we used in the workshop.

Ever since Ansel returned from Magitech Academy with a degree in hand, he'd turned into a different person.

Well, not different exactly. That wasn't the right word. Perhaps I was just now noticing what had been there all along. The years at the Academy had toned not only his mind but also his body, and I couldn't help noticing how much stronger he looked. When I looked at him, I didn't see the scared young teen I'd taken in anymore. I saw a man.

I saw an omega.

And that scared the shit out of me.

Not that it mattered now, though. I'd gone and lain with another omega in the heat of the moment, and now he was probably out there alone, and pregnant, and...

"Hold up," Arthur hissed, holding out a hand for us to stop. That snapped me out of my thoughts and back into the moment, my ears pricked up for any sound, my eyes scanning the horizon. I sniffed the air and didn't pick up anything unfamiliar.

As the team grew silent and listened, I heard what Arthur was talking about. Low voices murmured on the breeze, carrying over the rising hills to us in a garbled mix of sound. I strained my ears and wished I was in my shift. Dragon senses were a lot more perceptive, but shifting out in the open like this would definitely get us noticed.

I couldn't decipher many of the mumblings, but I did manage to pick up a few words, and they set my blood afire.

Attack.

Darkvale.

And then there was the name Elias...

We stared at one another, eyes wide. Elias was our resident Sorcerer, and a spy for the Firefangs. He'd sworn his loyalty. Did they know he was working for us? Or was there some deeper intent at play? I shivered at the thought.

Had the Sorcerer double-crossed us?

I listened harder but the voices carried away, gone like the ashes of a fire. The land was silent once more, and Arthur motioned for us to get off the road. We crept away from the open plains toward the cliffs while the scouts watched our back and the warriors held their weapons at the ready. None of us dared to breathe.

Arthur and Anya forged ahead once we'd cleared the area behind us and leapt down a series of ledges.

We followed on foot, still glancing behind us as we scrambled down the rock.

"What's going on?" Ansel hissed at me as we gathered on the small stone shelf. There wasn't a lot of room and we were all pressed together, which made my awareness of Ansel that much stronger. It was also the first time he'd spoken to me since the ball.

"Dunno," I mumbled back. "There's a troop nearby, heard 'em. We can hide out here till they pass."

The voices grew louder again and footsteps crackled down the dusty path. I held my breath and pressed myself against the wall, hoping they wouldn't notice us.

Just then, a rock tumbled from the precipice and splashed into the water below.

I let out a shaky breath and closed my eyes. Now we'd done it. No one moved.

The footsteps above us stopped and a voice rang out clear as crystal this time.

"I heard something."

Shit.

I shot my gaze to Marlowe, looking for direction. He gave an almost imperceptible shake of his head, commanding us to stay put.

"It came from over here," a second man's voice said. So there were at least two of them, four if I had to guess from the sound of their footsteps.

I heard them coming closer. We couldn't just stand here and get caught!

I shot a panicked glance at Marlowe and he tilted his head off the cliff and toward the splashing of the sea below. "Now," he mouthed, and we jumped.

We sailed through the air in free fall. Goddess, I'd missed that feeling. Wind whipped at my skin and the water rushed toward us below. I heard shouts from above but they all but faded into the background as I gave myself over to my shift. My muscles bulged and changed, my teeth lengthened into fangs, my mouth became a snout. Wings burst from my shoulder blades. I let out a roar and the sound of dragons filled the air.

Messing with a clan of dragon shifters? Bad idea.

I flapped my wings to gain altitude and saw the men that had almost uncovered our hiding place. They wore heat-resistant armor and glowing green gauntlets. They knew we were coming.

I wanted to blow them up right then and there, but then I heard a familiar screech. I whipped around. It was Ansel. He flailed and roared in a combination of pain and fear.

My heart leapt into my throat. *No! Not Ansel!*

I swiveled to find the source of the attack and locked eyes with a red-headed woman shrouded in a deep green robe. They had a fucking Sorcerer!

She swung her arms in a terrible arc and I knew I'd be next. Her energies surrounded Ansel and he quailed, limbs flailing frantically. He began to lose altitude.

I rushed forward, folding my wings to my sides to gain more speed. I didn't have time to think about it. All I knew was I had to save him.

Screams and roars of panic echoed in my ears. Steel clashed as both human and shifter collided. Marlowe lost his shift and fought hand to hand on the ground. The scouts kept their distance and blew flames from above.

I took it all in at a moment and filed it away. My protégé, my Ansel, was falling.

The wind roared in my ears as I fled toward him,

ignoring the spike of pain that lanced through my side. Had to get to him. Had to save him.

Ansel lost his shift in in mid-air, his frail body falling limp to the craggy beach below.

Time trickled by in slow motion. I focused on the sight of him, on my wings to carry me forward at just the right moment. At the last second before his body collided with the ground, I swooped beneath him and he landed on my back with a thud.

"I've got you!" I roared, skimming the surface of the waves. His weak arms clasped the pockets behind my wings and held on for dear life.

Tork...

This time I heard Ansel's voice not out loud but in my mind. I nearly fell out of the sky with the shock of it.

Ansel?

Everyone knew that fated mates had a mental connection, a Link on which they could speak telepathically. But we weren't mates. Far from it. There were reports of Links being formed between soldiers or other incredibly intimate relationships, but it was rare.

I heard Ansel again, and this time it was no hallucination.

Let's get those sons of bitches! He looped his legs around my torso and tightened his grip. A shiver of pride, purpose, and pleasure flowed through my every vein. I'd never felt anything like it before. It was like breathing fire, only times a thousand. My every cell vibrated with light and life and power.

I didn't have time to think or question. Only to act.

Go! He cried, I roared in triumph.

We sailed through the air like the riders of old, the force of our bodies and souls combined like a multiplier. I appraised the field at a glance—Marlowe grappled with what looked to be their leader while the scouts circled above and burned a ring of fire into the earth, preventing any escape.

Kari rejoined the fray, facing off against the sorcerer while Rex scavenged through their wagon of supplies.

First matter of business, the Sorcerer. With her neutralized we could use our powers again.

You gonna be okay if I shift back? I spoke to Ansel, still reveling in the knowledge that he could hear me.

Yeah, I'm good. Put me down.

I won't leave you, I promised, and we alighted on the cliff face. I took advantage of the Sorcerer's momentary distraction to shift back to human and run toward her full speed. I caught her in a tackle and she crumpled to the ground, eyes wild and teeth bared. She dug her knife-like nails into my arms, leaving a trail of fresh blood. I grunted in pain.

Rex tossed Kari a metal spike that he'd found in their stores and she leveled it at the Sorcerer's throat.

The mage narrowed her eyes at me, spittle forming on her lips. "You wouldn't kill me. Neither of you."

"Try me," Kari hissed, pressing the sharp point against her exposed skin.

"You're coming with us," I told her. "Or you can die. Your choice."

She snarled at me but there wasn't much she could do with the two of us restraining her.

I heard a shout and a thud from behind us and I nodded to Kari. "Hold her!"

I gave the Sorcerer a last withering look and released my grip, spinning around. I saw with horror that Marlowe lay on the ground unmoving and his attacker lunged at me with wide, angry eyes. He swung his blade toward what would have been my back if I hadn't moved at that exact moment. I feinted to the side and grabbed a vial from my hip, throwing the contents in his face. He screamed and I wrinkled my nose at the smell of burning flesh. His sword clattered to the ground and I lunged to pick it up, still on my guard.

Ansel ran to Marlowe's side as the scouts circled closer.

I held my wounded ribs and rounded on Rex, digging through the wagons and totally unguarded.

Look out for Marlowe, I'll cover Rex.

Deal.

I coughed as the fumes from the reagent burned my nose. I spent a long time gathering that. Didn't expect to use it to burn a man's face off, but hey, improvise.

"Find anything?" I asked Rex breathlessly as he looked up.

"There's a whole load of stuff here, looking like some parts for their automatons too. We need to get somewhere safe and study it."

"Can do. Is the wagon intact?"

"Looks like it."

"Good, let's get out of here."

I looked to the sky and signaled to the scouts. They circled lower now, back into the range of the Sorcerer's abilities. Though Kari held her hostage, she could still do a lot of damage if things got out of hand.

Arthur settled to the ground first, shifting back to human form as he ran to Marlowe's side. Anya joined me and Rex, a breathless look of terror in her eyes.

"There's more," she breathed. "A lot more. There's an unoccupied cave not far south but we gotta be careful."

My gut clenched and I motioned to Rex. "Pack up everything you can and follow me."

Ansel and Arthur helped Marlowe to his feet, unsteady but very much still alive. I let out a breath of relief. Thank the Goddess.

"Come on!" I waved to my team. "We've got to get settled before nightfall."

Anya led the way with me and Rex close behind. Ansel and Arthur took up the rear as they helped Marlowe along and Kari dragged the Sorcerer with her, still angling a knife at her throat if she dared try anything.

I kept my eyes peeled for any signs of movement as we moved toward the cave. Nothing save for the screech of sea birds and the smell of salt on the air.

I glanced back at Ansel more than once. Just to make sure he was all right, I told myself, but there was something else there too.

What had happened to us back there? Why could I suddenly hear him in my mind? And what was that power I felt flowing through my every cell when we touched?

"Stay on your guard," Anya reminded me, and I kept close to her with my sword drawn, just in case.

As the dry plains gave way to hills and then the rise of mountains, the air cooled and the birds disappeared. It happened as sudden as walking through a veil. This was no place for life. No place for anyone. We crested a hill and the land stretched out around us as stony spires reached toward the sky. The ground hardened and cracked from sun or from some other force I couldn't tell. A crow perched on a petrified tree branch, staring straight at us with his glassy eyes.

Caw!

I hated crows.

"You sure this is the right way?" I quickened my steps to catch up with Anya. She lengthened her spyglass and peered through it for a moment, her lips pursed. She collapsed it and turned to me, pointing.

"There, see that?"

I tried to follow her finger but all I could see was the rough outline of the oncoming mountains. The terrain all flowed together and made it hard to pick out any individual pieces.

She grabbed my shoulder and pulled me toward her, so I could see where she'd been standing. "Straight ahead." Anya handed me the spyglass to take a look. Before she relinquished her grip she narrowed her eyes and added, "Don't drop it."

I extended the spyglass and closed one eye, trying to make out what she'd seen on the horizon.

And there it was. Barely noticeable even with a spyglass, a darkened area between two rocky crags looked back at me. A smattering of white stone surrounded the entrance but I could not see any further within. It was well out of the way, through, and obscure enough we wouldn't be stumbled upon for the night. "How long?" I asked.

"Flying, we'd be there in no time." She shrugged. "But with our cargo," she nodded toward the hostage Sorcerer, "I wouldn't risk it."

I let out a breath. "How long on foot?"

"If we hurry? Till nightfall."

"Noted."

I hung back to relay the message to the warriors. Some of the color had returned to Marlowe's face but he still walked with a limp. If we were caught that off guard by a surprise attack, the chances for finding and neutralizing the automaton didn't look good.

"How are we doing back here?" I asked, noting that Ansel's shoulders sagged under the weight of helping Marlowe along. "Why don't you let me take over for a bit? Go help Anya."

Ansel's face twisted. "I can handle myself."

"I know you can, I just..." I wrung my hands. "Fine. Whatever."

"I could use a break," Arthur said, stretching his arms. "I need to go check in with Anya anyway." He gave me a queer look and extricated himself. He hurried off before I could ask what he meant by it.

My heart skipped a few beats in my chest. Something weird was going on between Ansel and I, and having to be in forced proximity while we headed for the cave? Not exactly what I'd had in mind.

"Sure," I said tonelessly, and I stepped in to loop Marlowe's shoulder over my own.

"I'm fine," Marlowe complained. "Stop treating me like an omega."

Ansel bristled at that. "You're hurt. Alpha or omega, doesn't matter. you need medical attention."

"It's nothing," he brushed off. "Really. I'm just slowing you down."

"No Firefang left behind," I reminded him, and we carried on in tense silence.

5

ANSEL

Talk about awkward.

Here I was, trying to ignore the feelings I got around my mentor, and now we were stuck together helping our commander Marlowe along. I focused on the task at hand and tried not to meet his gaze.

But I couldn't get him out of my mind.

What had happened back there was incredible. Beyond anything I'd ever felt or heard of. I didn't know how to explain it, but it looked like we were gonna have to have a talk sooner rather than later.

My stomach roiled at the thought and a wave of nausea passed. I heaved a little, doubling over as Marlowe stumbled. Tork appeared at my side instantly.

"You okay?" He asked, placing a hand on my shoulder. There was that spark again, the electricity that crackled between us like a live wire every time we touched.

"Fine," I muttered and wiped my mouth. "Got a little shaken up back there is all. Don't worry about it."

Tork narrowed his eyes in that "I don't believe you" look, but didn't press. Thank the Goddess for that. We resumed our positions and carried on across the wilds.

What he didn't know couldn't hurt him, I told myself as I cradled my upset belly with one hand. But the alpha I saw that night, the way I'd given myself to him...

Something like that couldn't stay a secret for long, especially if I was—I gulped—pregnant.

We arrived at the cave under the last vestiges of sunlight. Thankfully the trip had been mostly uneventful after the ambush on the road, but that didn't mean we could let our guards down.

No, all of us were tired, sore, and totally on edge.

We still had our hostage Sorcerer, after all. And although Marlowe gained color with each step, I still worried for him.

I worried for everyone. Part of being an omega, I guess.

After the scouts cleared the cave for us to enter, I set about building wards for the door to make sure no one would stumble upon us in the night. With a little bit of magic-infused metal and a sweeping sensor no bigger than a fingertip, I could track movements in a wide radius around the doorway. They were a simpler version of the same wards I used to protect Darkvale, only on a more impromptu scale.

I knew they'd brought me along for that reason. Even if I hadn't volunteered, they likely would have drafted me all the same. I was the only one that knew all the inner workings of the wards and how to build the magitech shields to keep out prying eyes. And for us on this kind of mission, staying out of sight was crucial.

I didn't mind the work. No, I relished the chance to throw myself into something other than my jumbled thoughts and the tug of my dragon toward someone I knew I couldn't have.

When I got home, I realized as I wiped my brow, I'd have to seek out my real mate. He'd want to start a family, no doubt. Heat or not, I couldn't deny the feeling of connection I'd experienced that night in the alpha's arms.

Heats were nothing new for an omega like me. I should have known better. But even before it came on, my dragon awakened at the sight of the alpha at the snack table. Even behind the mask and costume, it knew. This one was mine.

I shook my head and tightened the last bolt, fastening the new wards to each side of the cave entrance. With a mechanical buzzing sound, they activated and a barely visible sheen of light laced between them like a force field. I waved my hand through the entrance and they turned red, letting out an awful klaxon of sound. I flinched at the noise, even though I knew it was coming.

"Keep it down, won't you?" Rex muttered. He crouched over a circular indentation in the ground where he'd piled firewood. "Do you want to alert every living thing in a mile radius?"

"You'd rather we wait till something comes to eat us for dinner to see if it works or not?" I shot back. While he was a talented engineer, Rex played a little too fast and loose for my liking.

Rex grumbled into the fire and sparks flew from his mouth, catching the dry wood at once. It didn't take long for the pile of kindling to become a merry crackling fire, spreading some much needed warmth to my tired bones.

Long shadows flickered on the walls as we settled in for the night.

Anya distributed dinner in the form of dried jerky and rice cakes that tasted like dirt. I choked it down all the same with a splash of water from my skin—didn't realize how ravenous I was.

When was the last time I'd eaten, anyway?

The Sorcerer sat in chains near the fire, watching us with a sullen expression as she chewed on one of the cakes Kari had offered her. She was calmer now, her shoulders slumped in resignation as she stared into the flames. Kari fitted her with a set of sublimation shackles to quell her powers, then set to the task of interrogating her.

Dinner gurgled in my stomach and I worried that I might not keep it down. More unsettling still was the thought that perhaps this was more than just a stomachache.

I prepped my bedroll for the night and little by little movement died down. Everyone was tired, and dawn would come early. When it did, we had to be ready to go.

I fell asleep to the crackle of the fire and the rustle of the wind through the trees.

———

When I opened my eyes again, the fire had all but burnt itself out. It glowed in a lump of burning embers, throwing warm slants of light across the cave walls. As I opened my eyes a little further, I could see someone sitting in front of the fire, warming their hands. I couldn't tell quite who it was, the fire cast them in a dark silhouette, but I knew the answer anyway.

"Hey," I mumbled without moving from my bedroll. The man turned to look at me. Just as I'd expected, Tork's warm amber eyes looked back at me.

"You're awake," he said.

"Couldn't sleep."

Tork shrugged. "Me neither. One of us needs to keep watch, anyway."

I bristled at that. "The wards should do just fine. You know that."

"All the same." Tork stretched and avoided my gaze. He stared off into the distance, across the burning coals and up toward the small ventilation shaft through the ceiling. "I've got a lot on my mind," he admitted.

"Mind if I join you?" I whispered, moving quietly to not disturb the rest of the party.

"Sure," he said and patted a spot on the ground next to him.

I pulled the hide blanket away from my body and crawled over to the fire on hands and knees. Tork watched me each step of the way, his gaze hot on mine.

The tired embers glowed and sparks crackled from the coals up toward the sky and through the shaft to the sky beyond. Crickets chirped their persistent song outside, and the echoing hoot of an owl came at intervals.

"You ever been in the field like this?" Tork asked, giving me a sidelong glance. "They train you in that at your Academy?"

I blinked. Not once had Tork asked about my time at the Academy. I knew he was proud of me, sure. I knew he was glad to see me back home with degree in hand. But we never really talked about what went on there. And if I did tell him the truth, I doubted he'd ever believe it.

I shivered at the memories, even right next to the fire. "Not really," I replied, trying to sound casual. "More theory than practice. I learned a lot, sure, but—" I rubbed my arms and the gooseflesh there—"It's different in the real world, you know?"

"Don't I know it." Tork leaned back and propped himself on his elbows, his eyes still appraising me. For what, I didn't know.

We sat there in silence for what seemed like ages. The air stretched out in front of us, heavy with tension, with secrets, with that undeniable energy that linked us both. Finally, I couldn't take it anymore. I had to say something.

"We need to talk."

Tork raised an eyebrow. "About what?"

I swallowed. First things first. "About what happened back there. About the ambush. I was unprepared. I fell, I lost my shift, I..." I shook my head. "You caught me."

"What about it?" Tork asked slowly. "You're part of the clan. No Firefang left behind. I had to help."

I scoffed. "And that's all it was? Just doing your duty?" I wrung my hands. "Come on, Tork. That's not what I mean. I heard you, man. I *felt* you, for Glendaria's sake. What was all that about?"

Tork frowned and looked away now. Even in the dim light of the coals, his face flushed a shade I'd never seen before. Was he embarrassed?

"I don't know anything about that," Tork said finally. "Doesn't make any sense to me either. It's a mate thing, and we're not..."

The words spilled out now, flooding my tongue as the dam of pent up emotion broke. All the shame and guilt and fear washed over me like the sea, cold and just as drowning. "Speaking of mates," I continued in a low, strangled voice. "I need to tell you something."

Tork's throat bobbed as he listened. His hands were fists at his side, and I could practically feel the anxiety pouring off of him.

"I need to tell you something too," Tork sighed, rubbing the back of his neck.

I froze, my throat suddenly dry. Tork was a professional. He didn't get to be the head of demolitions and weapons science by fucking random strangers at balls.

When my dad died, Tork took me in and taught me everything he knew. And part of that was how to be a proper omega in society. How to serve the clan and do my duty. He taught me the importance of loyalty, respect, and honor.

I'd sullied all three.

I closed my eyes and thought again of my dad. Always there for me. Always strong. Powerful. Alpha. He sacrificed so much for me to have a good life. "I never thanked you properly," I said with a shaking voice. "For what you did for me. When my...When dad died." I choked out the last words.

"He was a good man," Tork said, his eyes far away. I wasn't the only one who'd lost someone. Veltar was his best friend, and the entire reason he'd become my godfather.

"He was," I agreed, remembering his smile, his scent, his strength when he'd pick me up and carry me around on his back. It was the closest thing to flying I'd experienced before I'd been able to shift myself.

63

I blinked at the tears welling up in my eyes. I gave a choking chuckle. "Sorry," I murmured and wiped my face.

"No," Tork started, and reached out a hand toward me. Then he stopped in midair, as if thinking better of it. His hand fell, and so did my spirits. "No sorries necessary."

He paused for a moment, then added, "You're a good man too, Ansel."

When I looked up those glowing orbs were boring into mine, full of emotion and purpose.

I wanted to look away, but couldn't. It was like some otherworldly force held me in, drawing us together like iron filings to a magnet.

"I don't know about that," I whispered, my cheeks hot with guilt.

"Oh yeah?" This time Tork didn't resist. He reached forward and planted a hand on my chin. "Why's that?"

He tilted it up toward his own and my lips parted slightly. I was suddenly too aware of Tork's touch, the tingle in my lips, the shiver of pleasure that crawled all the way down my spine.

There was no way this could be happening. No way my body would respond this way. I'd worked with Tork for ages and he'd never affected me this way. Until...

The pieces clicked together and I scooted backwards, gasping for breath.

"It was you," I rasped, my voice cracking.

"It was I, what?" Tork crossed his arms. "English, please."

"That night, at the festival, it was you..."

Tork's eyes widened and his mouth hung open. He blinked as if seeing for the first time. "No..." He started. "No..."

"Does this look at all familiar to you?" I pulled out a single silver feather and dangled it next to my ear.

"It can't be..." Tork whispered, turning away. "It's not right. It's not honorable. Just think of what Veltar would have said!"

"Why can't it be right?" I pressed. The vibration in my soul resonated ever stronger now with the knowledge that this was my mate. Not some random stranger from a party. Tork. "Tell me you don't feel this between us." I laced his fingers with mine and he sucked in a breath, still avoiding my gaze.

"You're Veltar's son," he moaned. "I could never..."

"Don't you believe in fate?" I asked him, gesturing to the stars above.

"Never did," Tork responded in a gruff tone.

"Ever since I was a kid, I heard that Glendaria has someone for us all out there. Our destiny. Our fated mate. Sometimes it just takes a while to find them, even if they've been in front of your face the whole time."

Tork frowned and chewed his lip. "I don't know what to think anymore."

"You felt our powers combine!" I beseeched him now, my voice raising by a hair. "You felt the mating pull, same as I. You heard our Link. We're mates, Tork. I'm sure of it."

The fire crackled on, spewing sparks and smoke toward the ceiling. Neither of us spoke for a long time—we sat there as the information sunk in. Tork didn't yank his hand away from mine. We sat there, fingers linked, and stared at the flickering coals in silence.

"I..." Tork opened his mouth at last, then a loud snore cut him off.

We both turned at the noise and saw Marlowe rolling about in bed, snoring and mumbling to himself.

"Go away, why don't you...I'm busy." He snorted and threw a hand over his face. "Making...flower crowns...gotta...be pretty." He snored again then rolled over on his stomach and back to sleep.

We glanced at one another and couldn't hold back our giggles anymore. My body shook with repressed laughter. Marlowe was never gonna live that down. For that moment, we weren't on a deadly mission to save Darkvale and all we held dear. We were just friends, enjoying one another's company, the heat of the fire, and the antics of our clan members.

Tomorrow's struggles couldn't touch us. The war loomed far off like a misremembered dream. Tension and anxiety melted away from my bones and we sat there, leaning on one another.

My mentor. My friend. My mate.

Maybe this would work out after all.

6

TORK

I opened my eyes to a new dawn, and a new revelation along with it.

I couldn't believe it. Didn't want to believe it. It hovered in my mind like mist, and I feared if I grasped at it too tightly, it might fly away for good.

Ansel...my mate?

When I looked over at the sleeping omega beside me, I knew it was the truth. Doubt and tension faded away to leave only a warm, grateful feeling in its place.

Mine to behold. Mine to protect.

I couldn't deny what I'd felt between us, sure, but I couldn't shake the guilt that seized me like a vise.

Was I confused? Definitely. Was I aroused at the same time? Hell yeah.

When we touched, my dragon responded in a way I'd never felt before. When we fought together, our powers combined. By standing together, we became greater than ourselves.

But whatever this was, exploring it would have to wait. We had an important mission to do, and this trick of ours just might be the thing to turn the tides.

———

The sun peeked through the shimmery veil of the entrance, casting the rest of the clan in a warm glow. My clansmen stirred one by one, righting themselves for the day.

Only, one was missing.

"The Sorcerer!" Kari cried out. "She's gone!"

"What?" Marlowe snapped, rubbing the sleep from his eyes. "How?"

"Dunno," Kari wrung her hands.

"Check your packs, everyone. Make sure she didn't steal anything."

That got the clan moving, and I raced to check my stores with my heart in my throat. Ansel made better wards than anyone I knew, and they would have gone off if the Sorcerer tried to escape. Must have found another way out. I grimaced and pawed through my supplies, letting out a breath. Everything in its place.

"We're good," Rex announced.

"All clear for us," Arthur echoed, nodding at Anya.

"Then what happened?" Marlowe asked, folding his arms. "She may be a Sorcerer but she didn't just vanish in a puff of smoke. Ansel, check the wards."

"On it, Commander." Ansel was already up and moving, peering at each of the mechanical sensors he'd attached to the doorway. He leaned in close, staring at them through a magnifying crystal, then shrunk back. "They're intact, sir. Nothing's come this way."

"There must be another exit," I suggested.

"Shall we track her?" Arthur asked.

Marlowe let out a string of curses and finally a long ragged breath. "Let her go. We've got bigger matters to deal with."

The clan grew silent at Marlowe's edict. All of us, me included, were thinking about what might happen if the Sorcerer got back to her buddies and told them where we were.

"We pack up. We get out of here. We find the infernal contraption we came for, and we do our duty."

Marlowe's voice echoed off the walls and sent a chill down my spine.

"Very well," Arthur said with a nod. "You heard him, get moving!"

———

Packing our things didn't take long—we'd traveled light to begin with, and pretty much crashed as soon as we reached the cave last night.

The trouble came when Kari distributed the morning rations.

Everyone else was on their way out, but Ansel hung back. He dragged himself across the cave like it cost him incredible effort, his eyes far away. Despite the professional front he'd put on this morning, I could see now that his skin held a sickly pallor and he struggled to nibble on the square of ration provided. His forehead shone with a delicate sheen of sweat, even though it was far from warm out. When he doubled over and started heaving, I rushed to his side at once.

I held his hair back as he gagged and shook, watching with horror as he ejected the past day's meals. It was then that I caught the scent that had been flickering in and out for days. It was then that I finally put the pieces together and realized.

Ansel wasn't just my mate. He was pregnant.

My chest squeezed and my heart raced as I held him. My dragon protested noisily in my chest. Alpha instincts took over and I brushed a hand through his hair, helping him wipe his mouth and right himself. "You okay?" I asked softly.

"Yeah, I'm fine, I'm just..."

"Pregnant," I finished, looking him dead in the eye. "Why didn't you say something?"

"Didn't know," Ansel whispered, staring at the ground. "Not for sure, anyway."

"It's for sure, all right. My dragon won't shut up about it."

That got a little laugh out of him, and I couldn't help smiling as well. "We've got to get you back to Darkvale." I took hold of both his hands. "It's not safe out here."

Ansel twisted out of my grasp, frowning. "What, cause I'm an omega?"

"No, cause you're pregnant. If something happened to you..."

"I knew the risks, Tork. I chose to come along."

"Yeah, but that was before..." I put my hands on my hips. He was being so difficult!

"And who's going to man the wards if I'm gone?" Ansel shot back, slinging his bag over his shoulder and turning for the exit where the rest of the clan waited.

I groaned and rolled my eyes. "Look, you're an adult, and you can make your own decisions, but think about the baby, Ansel. Our baby."

That seemed to get through to him and his face softened, his muscles slackened. He sagged and looked a little green again until I put a steadying hand on his shoulder.

Trust me? I asked over our newly-formed Link, knowing that he'd hear me in his mind.

Ansel leaned forward and rested his head on my chest as I held him close.

I made a promise to Veltar to keep him safe. And that's just what I would do.

"Guys, come on! I found something!" Arthur's voice drew me out of my trance and Ansel broke away from me at once, jogging to catch up.

I shook my head and followed after him.

He never had been too good with authority. Should have known.

———

We crested a hill to look down on a sandy plain below. Between the rocks and weeds there was a strange circle burned into the earth, a sort of sooty black halo. The ground inside the ring bore no such burn marks. It was fine and crumbly, freshly turned.

"Someone's been here," Anya said, bending down to brush at the dirt. "Whoever was here was trying to cover something up. And they didn't do a very good job of it."

We brushed at the perimeter and the hastily dumped dirt fell away, exposing the scorched earth beneath.

What was even more interesting was the trap door concealed there.

"What do you think?" Marlowe asked me.

I sniffed the air and caught the scent of iron and oil and soot.

"That's them, all right. Same kind of residue we found on the automaton."

"I say we go in," Kari suggested, drawing her weapon and kicking the last debris away from the hinges. "Bet they're hiding."

I remembered the last time I'd gone to explore an unknown tunnel and shivered. I would have died down there if it weren't for Nik and Ansel finding us. "You all have masks? You know what happened last time."

Kari strapped a filter to her face and tossed a few out to the other members of the team.

"Someone's gonna need to stand watch. If we don't come back..."

I nodded. No rushing in to save the day this time. Last time I tried that, I nearly got both Marlowe and I killed. "Ansel and I will stay."

Ansel opened his mouth like he was about to retort but I shot him a glare and he quieted down.

"Very well," said Marlowe as he strapped a mask over his face. "You see anything out of the ordinary, anything at all, you call us out and we'll be right there."

"Same goes for you," I nodded to him and clapped him on the back. "Glendaria go with you."

"And with you," he echoed, and heaved open the dusty trap door.

"You know what to do," Marlowe reminded me, then each of them disappeared down the hole and out of sight.

Then it was just the two of us.

Volunteering Ansel to stand watch with me had a twofold purpose. I didn't want him to get into any more danger than needed, but I also needed a moment of privacy to speak with him about this whole mating thing.

But no sooner had the trapdoor thudded closed than we heard a metallic grinding sound behind us. I whirled and what I saw approaching took my breath away.

Nearly twenty feet tall, a cobbled together monstrosity of wires and metal stood there, gazing down on us with shining white eyes. I saw spots and took a few steps back, spinning around to wrench at the trapdoor.

"It's a trap!" I yelled through the wood. "Get out here! Get out here now!"

I pulled at the door with all my might, but it wouldn't budge.

Trapped.

I sucked in a breath and rushed to put myself between the monster and Ansel. He would have to go through me first.

It creaked its way toward us, smelling like smoke and sulphur. Ansel grabbed my hand and linked our fingers until I felt the sparks of connection rage through me once more.

"Let's do this," he said, and I squeezed his hand in return.

I dug into my bag for one of the portable mines I'd

brought along. Just in case, of course. They packed a mighty punch when activated, but I had to get close enough to the thing to place one. And if I messed up, it might blow on me instead.

"Stay with me," I commanded Ansel, who already wove a tenuous thread of silk between his fingers, lashing it together and whispering an inscription into the rope. It shone with a pale blue light for a moment, then faded away.

"Here," he offered an end of the reinforced strand to me, and when I didn't immediately respond, he said, "Tie it to the mine, we can use it like a lasso."

"Genius," I said excitedly and tied the end through an opening in the mine's mechanical underbelly. I had to hope the string wouldn't trigger the switch in the meantime.

"We need some kind of adhesive," I muttered, digging through my stores as the automaton grew closer.

Sleeping draught...explosive merryroot...no, no, no.

Then my fingers closed around a small glass vial I forgot I even had. There!

I pulled out the vial and tossed the cork aside. A thick brown substance rested within, congealed with age.

"Terra sap," Ansel breathed, "Brilliant."

I shook the vial vigorously over the mine's backside, but the liquid stayed put. "Come on," I grumbled, shaking it harder.

"Was Terra sap the one that thins like honey when you warm it up, or the one that explodes?" Ansel looked to me with wide eyes.

"We're about to find out," I said after placing it on the ground, and let out a jet of flame.

The substance bubbled and boiled almost instantly, but the mixture remained stable, thank the Goddess, I grabbed it, burning my fingers in the process, and dumped the sticky sap in a puddle onto the backside.

"There we go," I grinned and gave Ansel a high five. "Self adhesive lasso mine. Easy."

"Let's see if it works first—duck!"

I threw myself to the ground just in time. A sharpened metal bolt whizzed over my head so close I could feel the air rush through my hair. Any closer and I would have gotten a face full of metal. I rolled to the side and regained my feet. Adrenaline coursed through my veins and pushed away all second thoughts, all fear, all pain. I swung the contraption over my head in a circle once, twice, three times. It gained speed and the mechanics within grated, then whirred into action.

"Armed and ready," I muttered to myself, then

narrowed my vision to the huge metal man in front of me. I had one chance to get this right.

The automaton reeled back and pummeled the ground with both fists, sending a shockwave out in a huge radius. The ground shuddered beneath my feet and I miscalculated my target, letting the rope free a moment too soon. I could only watch with wide eyes as it sailed through the air.

With a splat it came to rest on the beast's knee, and thank the Goddess, it held! A far cry from the headshot I'd been aiming for, but good enough.

"Move!" I barked at Ansel, covering him.

The monster tilted its head and looked, confused at the whirring, beeping contraption attached to its leg. The noise grew louder, the beeping faster. I squeezed my eyes shut.

Boom.

I shielded Ansel with my body as the explosion shook the ground and roared in my ears. Heat seared my back and metal crashed to the ground, then all was silent. When I turned around to look, my heart dropped even further.

The blast had torn off the thing's leg, but it was still moving! Those shining white eyes locked onto us with even more malice than before, and it reached out with its clawed hands, scraping through the dirt toward us.

Ansel stumbled back a few steps with a wail.

What now? I raced through my mind trying to come up with a solution. I only had that one mine left, and to detonate anything else this close to the entrance would cave in the tunnel. The rest of the team would be trapped.

We needed to lure it away.

"Hey pea brain!" Ansel taunted. He set off at a run in the opposite direction, waving his arms madly. The automaton took notice and dragged its head away from me to zero in on Ansel's fleeing form.

No!

"Ansel you idiot!" I bellowed, but my voice was lost in the metallic screech as the automaton let out another razor-sharp bolt, whizzing right toward Ansel's skull.

Watch out!

He swerved to the left at the last second and the arrow buried itself, quivering, in the dirt.

He was moving too fast for explosives and it was too big for my puny sword. I had to protect my mate, at any cost.

Dragon power flowed through me as I began to shift

and leave my human body behind. Wings sprouted from my shoulder blades, my teeth lengthened into lethal daggers, my legs and arms grew stronger, deadlier, faster. I let out a roar that shook the ground beneath us and lumbered toward him, the both of us comparable in size now.

Dragon versus giant robot.

Never thought I'd see the day.

I had one massive advantage over the crippled automaton, however.

I wasn't missing a leg.

I barreled into the contraption full on, the shock reverberating through my scales. We crashed to the ground together and the air was a haze of metal and spikes and screeching. I let out a column of flame right at the things face. The metal withstood the heat, and I kept flaming, using all my energy and spark. I was going to roast this son of a bitch no matter what it took. He was threatening my omega!

The metal glowed a bright red and seared through my armored flesh as I ran out of steam. A compartment near the head sprung and steam billowed out.

Inside the giant robot was...a man.

His face was bright red with sweat and exertion. Blood

dripped from his forehead and he regarded me with a delirious grin. Then I saw it.

Holding the collar of the man's shirt together was a metal buckle with an insignia I only faintly recognized. When I did, though, it took my breath away.

A cog with a lance through it. The emblem of Steamshire.

"What are you doing here?" I demanded, looming over the wreckage and pinning him to the ground. "What business does Steamshire have with the Firefangs?"

The man gave me a grim smile showing a few missing teeth. His eyes flashed. He knew something I didn't. "You're too late," he coughed. "You have no idea what's coming, do you? Filthy animals."

"Say that again!" I bellowed and prepared to strike.

"Wait!" Ansel cried, rushing toward us. I held my tongue.

"What?" I spat. "This man, this *human*, seeks to undo us all!"

"Let him speak. He's no use to us dead."

My dragon grumbled deep in my chest but I relented. Still kept a wary eye trained on his weapons, though.

"No longer will your kind threaten us with your

powers," the Steamshire man rasped. "Turns out we have powers of our own."

He pressed a button on the inside of his suit. I didn't have time to react. The automaton, human and all, exploded in a storm of fire and debris, throwing us backward with the blast. My ears rung, deafened. I knocked my head on the ground. The world spun.

But all I could think about, all I could see, was Ansel's still body spread out on the ground beside me.

I crawled over to where he lay on his stomach and flipped him over. Good, he was still breathing.

"Ansel!" I called both out loud and through our Link. "Ansel, talk to me!"

I shook him by the shoulders but he didn't move. My pleas remained unanswered.

"Ansel, baby, no!" Tears sprung to my face now as I leaned over him.

There was a wooden knock from beside me and I turned to see the trapdoor shuddering. The blows came again. I held my breath. Either it was the rest of my clan coming back to the surface, or it was whatever fell beasts had befallen them within.

I heaved Ansel into my arms and stood on shaky legs. The pounding came again and the wood splintered with a crash. A hand shot out, then another.

It was them.

I let out a breath. Marlowe surfaced first, dragging himself back onto the earth. He leaned down and offered a hand up to the rest of the men and women, each of them clambering out of the tunnel dirty, bloody, and totally spent.

When Marlowe saw the scattered debris, he froze. Then he looked to me, still holding Ansel in my arms.

"Goddess, don't tell me..." He said weakly.

"They snuck up on us." I grimaced. "Doesn't look like you fared much better."

Marlowe ignored my question. He nodded to Ansel warily. "Is he...?"

"No," I said a little more forcefully than I intended. The reptilian rasp of my dragon forced its way into my voice as I thought of my mate, my Ansel, passing from this world into the next. "He's knocked out, is all."

"You ran into one of...them?" Marlowe eyed the wreckage.

"We did, and it wasn't pretty. Permission to return to Darkvale, sir. We need to warn the others."

He brushed off his clothes and looked around at the team, then at me and Ansel. "You're taking him back too, I wager?"

"I am," I said protectively, holding him closer. "He's not only hurt, Commander. He's pregnant."

Marlowe's eyebrows raised so high on his forehead I thought they'd fly off. "My word."

"I'm taking him home," I said. It was more of a statement, not a question. If I got in trouble, if they labeled me AWOL, I didn't care. It didn't matter. My mate was in trouble.

"Does his mate know?" Marlowe asked softly, still staring at us in awe.

"He does now," I confirmed with a wink, and pushed off the ground with my strong back legs into the air. Ansel clung to my back and as I gained altitude, I watched the gaping faces below.

Let them talk. The dragon and the alpha in me had other plans.

7

ANSEL

Wind rushed through my hair and tickled my nose. I was afloat on clouds of cotton, resting peacefully while the world flowed around me.

Achoo!

I sneezed and jolted awake so violently I nearly fell off Tork's back.

I gripped onto the pockets behind Tork's wings for dear life and squeezed him with my thighs, ignoring the aching pain that sprouted up all over my body. I blinked my eyes once, twice, three times.

Then I made the mistake of looking down.

My stomach rebelled once more and I heaved, bile burning the back of my throat.

You're awake, I heard Tork's voice in my mind. It soothed me, just knowing he was there.

Where are we, I sent back. *What are you...*

I'm taking you home.

I swallowed past the lump in my throat and renewed my grip. My mate's wings flapped easily, gracefully, riding each current of wind and floating through the clouds with ease. The world was nothing but a speck of tiny trees and houses below. Little black dots like ants were the sign of people.

Images of metal and fire and ash flickered through my mind again. I was there. I was next to him. We finally found one of the mysterious automatons. And Steamshire was behind it.

Then he self destructed, I flew through the air, and then...

I was here.

I shook my head and blinked against the tears in my eyes.

The mission, I breathed. *Tork, the mission! What happened to everyone else?*

Some things are more important than the mission, Tork assured me. *I made a promise, and I intend to keep it.*

But, I started.

Tork was never one to run from a fight. Never. And to think he'd do that for me?

We've got to get back to Darkvale and warn them. If we can get there in time and tell Lucien to call in reinforcements, we might have a chance.

He had a point. Just one of those things was difficult enough to take down. If we were up against a whole army of them? I heaved again, only dry hacking sobs this time.

Hang on, Tork urged me. *We're getting you home as soon as possible. We're gonna see Doctor Parley when we get back. And then we've got work to do.*

I grumbled, but couldn't do much to resist. I was too weak to shift, and exhaustion draped over me like a blanket, warm and inviting. Sleep beckoned me once more and I settled into the warm, smooth scales on Tork's back.

"Do you smell chicken?" I mumbled, sniffing the air. "Cause I do."

Tork's body shook with laughter. "What are you talking about? You get knocked on the head too?"

"No," I insisted. The smell was there, all right. I could nearly taste it on my tongue, it was so strong. "Chicken," I continued. My mouth watered at the thought. "Hot, greasy, delicious....do you think we can get some fried chicken back in Darkvale? I'm so hungry."

Tork didn't stop chuckling for a good while. I lay sleepily on his back, glad to have amused him. "You always were a handful," he muttered. "And yes, when we get back, you can have all the chicken you want."

"Good," I mumbled, half asleep now. "You sure everyone will be all right? Now that we've left?"

It would be a lie to say I didn't feel a little guilty. But we had an important mission, perhaps more important than our work in the field. If shit was gonna hit the fan, Darkvale needed to know sooner rather than later. And that's where we came in.

"Here, I'll show you," Tork offered. "Open your mind, see what I see..."

I felt the same rush of power and energy as he reached out across our Link. Then the world faded away and a new landscape built itself up around me.

———

It was the cave we'd spent the night in. I could see myself, still sleeping. Marlowe approached Tork as they readied themselves for the day and gestured for him to come closer, speaking in a low tone only he could hear.

"I don't know much about people. I definitely don't

know much about relationships. But I saw the way you leaned on each other last night."

I snorted and my face flushed as I thought about our secret night together. Marlowe had been sleeping...or so we had thought.

Believe me, I was mortified too, Tork said in my mind. The scene continued to play out, and I looked on in wonder.

"It's not so unusual, you know." Marlowe put a hand on Tork's shoulder. "Glendaria has plans for all of us, even ones we don't understand sometimes." He stared at the ground for a moment, chewing his lip, then spoke again. "For what it's worth, I think Veltar would be proud that such a strong, capable alpha was fated to his son."

I couldn't see Tork's face well, but the corners of his mouth twitched up in a silent smile.

"Better than some prick that would abuse him, right?" Marlowe shrugged. "I know you'll do right by him. You'd do right by anyone. You're a good man, Tork."

Tork nodded his head. "My thanks."

"If what we've seen and heard is true, Darkvale is gonna need a lot more men."

"Don't I know it." Tork sighed. A moment passed between them, then Tork bowed his head and pressed his hands together. "Thank you, Commander. I won't let you down."

"Glendaria go with you, Tork."

"And with you, brother."

The walls faded away, the voices no more than mumbles in the background now. Tork and Marlowe dissipated like mist, and then they were gone.

———

When I could see again, the great towering walls came into view. The shimmering dome of Darkvale glowed and sparkled in the sunlight, and I'd never been so glad to see it.

"Come on, Ansel. We're home."

8

———

ANSEL

"Looks like you've got a baby dragon on the way. Two, if I'm not mistaken."

"Two?" I said hoarsely. "Twins?"

"Looks like it," Dr. Parley nodded and stuffed some paperwork into a folder. "Don't worry about a thing, though. I've delivered babies for quite a few omegas now, no problems."

I gulped, still digesting the news. *Twins.*

I wasn't so sure I could handle one baby, but two? Good thing I was already sitting down.

Tork placed a hand on my shoulder to steady me and I leaned forward into his warmth.

"How are you doing?" He asked, rubbing small circles on my back.

"Okay," I mumbled. "Still hungry."

"Let's go home and get you that chicken." Tork held out a hand and I grabbed it, sliding off the observation table.

"Don't hesitate to let us know if there's any problems." Dr. Parley said as he handed Tork the folder. "And Ansel?"

"Yeah?" I turned to see his mischievous grin.

"Take it easy on him. Alphas go a little crazy during pregnancy too."

"Hey!" Tork retorted, but I just laughed and let him lead me out of the clinic.

With that out of the way, now we had to go see Lucien and tell him about the oncoming threat. My stomach roiled again at that.

"You sure you don't want to go home?" Tork asked, rubbing my back. "I can deal with Lucien myself. You need your rest."

"I'll be fine," I insisted. "I want to be there. I'm not gonna turn into some helpless omega just cause I'm pregnant, you know." I brushed his hand away.

"I wouldn't dream of it." Tork kissed my hand and we headed toward Lucien's office.

We opened the door to Lucien's office to a bit of familial chaos. Lucien hunched over his desk, trying to read a book, while Alec fought with little Corin to eat his food. The baby definitely had some dragon in him, I noted with a smile. He was a feisty one, knocking away Alec's hand at each turn.

Lucien looked up as we entered and tilted his head in confusion.

"You're back so soon. Is something wrong?"

"Yes...and no." Tork started. He cast an eye over the screaming child and gestured toward the door. "We should go somewhere private."

Lucien's throat worked and he gave us a terse nod. "Very well." He stood up from behind his desk and followed us to the door. "Around the corner to the left, there's a unused storage room I like to go and think sometimes."

When I entered the "storage room", I had the strangest sense of deja vu. It looked just like the room Tork and I had mated in, back at the Flower Festival. I shot him a glance and I saw the same secret gleam in his eye. I cleared my throat, hoping the blush hadn't reached too far up my cheeks, when Lucien came in behind us and shut the door.

"This will do," he said, brushing dust off the old armchairs and the futon. "Sit, sit. Tell me what's going on."

I took a deep breath and sunk into the cushions. Tork joined me and put a protective hand around my shoulder.

"Don't tell me you two have finally mated..." he grinned.

Finally? Was it that obvious?

"Yes," Tork said simply, to save me the embarrassment. "But that's not what's important right now. We've news from the field, and we need your help."

"I'm all ears." His voice remained even, his demeanor professional, but I could tell underneath there was an undercurrent of despair.

"We found the automaton," I began. I took a breath. "We found a lot more than that, too."

"There are more of them than we thought," Tork added with a furrowed brow. "They're operational, Lucien. Huge. Powerful. And we found out who's behind it all."

Lucien didn't respond, just watched us silently, his chin resting on his hands.

"It's Steamshire!" I blurted. "They're out for revenge." A chill passed through me.

This time the Clan Alpha shrunk back as if shocked by lightning. The color drained from his face. "Goddess preserve us," he muttered. "The humans...I'll need to tell Alec at once."

"There's more," Tork cautioned. "They're on their way here, now. We came back to warn you, to call in reinforcements. If we're going to make it through this, Darkvale needs backup."

Lucien rubbed the back of his neck and regarded us. "Diplomatic relations have been...strained, to say the least. But we've made contact with a tribe of elementals on our last journey, Alec and I. We'll reach out to them now, call them to our aid. Is Marlowe still in the field?"

"He's right behind us," Tork promised. "They'll be back soon."

"Well we must get to work, then," Lucien stood and brushed his hands on his pants. "There's no time to lose."

"You've got that right."

Lucien hurried to the door and ushered us out. "Thank you, Ansel. And you too, Tork. Your information may just save us all."

"It's my pleasure, Clan Alpha." Tork bowed his head. I did the same.

"Oh, and Ansel?" He added as an afterthought. "Congratulations."

He eyed me with a knowing grin, and then he was gone.

I wanted to go after him, to help call in the allies and do anything I could to prepare for the siege, but my body had other ideas. My head pounded and my limbs felt like bricks. I sunk back into the chair as soon as Lucien had left.

Tork didn't say anything, just took my hand. "Let's get you home."

Home, I thought with a smile.

"We'll go back to my place. It's closer. In the meantime, I'll see what I can do about those cravings."

For once, I didn't have the energy to challenge him.

———

I'd visited Tork's place many times, but none since returning from the Academy. It looked much as I'd left it, but everything seemed smaller than I'd remembered. I reminded myself that I'd been smaller too, back then. He sat me down on the bed and brought me a huge cream-colored blanket. I had to laugh at the ridiculousness of it all. Even though he was my godfather and mentor, he'd never been so fussy over me before.

I guessed Doctor Parley was right. Pregnancy drove more than just omegas crazy.

I wove my hands through the delicate stitches and wrapped myself from head to toe.

"Where'd you get something like this?"

"My grandmother made it. She was great at stuff like that. Used to always give it to me when I was sick."

I snickered at that. "I'm not sick, Tork. Just pregnant."

"I know. But I want you to have it."

I yawned and curled up in the blanket, my eyes drooping closed. Tork still rushed around at a pace that made me dizzy. Finally, I said something.

"What about you? You doing okay?"

"What?" He asked, looking up. "I'm fine."

"You've been spending all this time worrying over me, but what about you? I know you got hurt back there. I know you've been ignoring it. And they probably need you back at the lab, and..."

"Shhh," Tork cut me off as a knock sounded at the door.

My muscles tensed up involuntarily. "Who's that?"

"Special delivery." Tork made his way to the door and said his thank yous to the courier standing there. Even though I didn't have a clear line of sight to the doorway, I could smell my present before I saw it.

"Chicken!" I shouted.

"Just the way you like it." Tork placed the package down on the kitchen counter and unwrapped it. An entire steaming chicken looked back at me, glistening with grease and breading and herbs.

"Goddess, that smells good," I moaned, twisting in my seat.

"You wanna eat over there or come in here?" Tork asked as he plated the meat.

"I'm basically a blanket burrito right now, so..."

Tork chuckled. "Anything for my omega."

My face burned at that, but the lightness I felt in my heart more than made up for it.

I was his, and he was mine. This was what all the old songs spoke about. What people went to war over, what people died for.

Having a mate, a true mate, was the best feeling of my life. And getting to start a family with him?

Well, that was just the icing on the cake.

He rounded the couch and sat down next to me, handing me a plate and some utensils.

I paid them no mind—I was so hungry! I picked up the chicken leg and bit right into it. The juices exploded in my mouth and dribbled from my fingers and lips. I let out a moan. I could taste each herb, each bread crumb, each bite more than ever before. My taste buds had rocketed up along with my sense of smell, and I was in heaven.

Tork watched me and the discarded utensils with amusement. I didn't care.

"This is really good," I said between bites. "Thank you so much."

Tork beamed and tore into his own plate. "Looks like you needed it."

"Did I ever," I agreed, and we passed the evening with food and comfort.

———

I'd never felt so sated in my life.

Well, maybe except for my mating night.

Speaking of...

I glanced over at Tork, who was just finishing his meal.

"So..." I started, but the words stuck in my throat. This was all so sudden, for the both of us. I knew Tork was doing his best to be a good alpha and a good partner, but his initial apprehension still ate at me. What if he didn't really want to be mates? What if he regretted what we did?

"I know this has all happened so fast. And I know you weren't exactly, um, on board with it at first." My words trailed off as I peeked through my eyelashes at Tork. "I never had a chance to really ask you though. Are you...okay with all this? I don't want to force you into anything."

Tork wiped his mouth and put his plate aside. He took my hands in each of his, and those glowing amber eyes searched deep into mine.

"I made a promise to Veltar, the day he died." Tork's voice was reverent now, echoing all the way down to my soul. "I will admit that mating his son wasn't part of the deal. But the more I think about it, maybe it was. My dragon wants to take care of you, Ansel. Body and soul. I thought I was doing just that before, but then at the Flower Festival..." he stopped, pursing his lips. "I should never have taken advantage of you that night. And for that, I am sorry. But when our souls combine, Ansel, it feels right. It feels like maybe we *were* meant to be mates, after all. And I want that. I want you, and everything you are."

He leaned forward and kissed me, and every doubt faded away.

My dragon responded instantly, pulling me closer like a magnet as I returned the kiss, hot and fierce and demanding. His lips captured mine, his tongue teased me in an impossibly frustrating dance. I grasped the back of his head, pulling him closer as I shot my own tongue out. He growled with satisfaction, and then I was airborne.

Tork's strong arms lifted me off the ground and into his embrace, his kisses landing on my face, my neck, my chin. He carried me down a hallway as I clung tightly. Through a doorway with a cloth banner for a door, and we were in his bedroom.

He let me go right over the bed and I bounced into the plush mattress, the air whooshing out of me. No sooner had I sunk into the mound of pillows than Tork was on me, his shirt thrown to the side in a heap.

This time I was in control. This time I would feel everything. Remember everything.

I ran my hands down the muscled planes of his chest and stomach, arching my back upwards.

He batted my hands away and ground his groin into

mine. If my cock hadn't already been hard and begging for release, it was now. It strained against my pants, aching and twitching at each movement of his hips. I reached a hand down to my fly but he batted it away again.

"Let me do it," he rumbled, and made quick work of the zipper. My pants came away and my cock was left throbbing against my underwear. Tork tugged at my shirt and I obliged, throwing it over my head. I wound my arms around his neck and sunk back down into the bed, bringing him with me.

His arms wrapped around my back and kneaded the tight area between my shoulder blades. I groaned in delight and my dragon responded in kind, the wings tickling at that very spot, eager to come out.

"Careful," I breathed, looking up at him with a mischievous eye. "You're gonna make me shift."

"Maybe I want that," he purred, moving his lips down to my collar bone and leaving a series of nips that took my breath away.

"Tork," I sighed, throwing my head back as he moved lower.

"Yes?" He asked, raising an eyebrow.

I grit my teeth and fisted my hands in the sheets. He had to know what he was doing to me! My heart thudded like a war drum, each pulse of blood heading straight for my cock and leaving me in a breathless, lightheaded trance.

When I didn't answer he continued his downward assault, stopping to nip and kiss at my hips and thighs. He orbited around the area of my most essential need, giving everywhere attention but my hard and leaking cock. He knew what he was doing, and he knew how it made me feel. My shuddered moans were proof of that. When he finally closed his lips over the head of my cock, it was like fireworks. Literal fireworks.

Tork's mouth was hot and greedy, sucking at my tender flesh. He bobbed up and down, his strong hands moving to cup my balls. I gasped at that—because it was unexpected, and because it felt so damn good. That in tandem with the way he pleased my cock with his mouth...I nearly came right then and there.

"Stop," I gasped through gritted teeth. Tork looked up at me. "I don't want to come...not yet...please..."

My staff slipped out of his mouth with a pop and he kissed his way back up my torso before whispering in my ear, "No. You're not going to come until you've had all you can take, and more."

I shuddered at the thought, but my cock had other ideas. It twitched again, leaking precum. My dragon fell into a full on frenzy and I couldn't stop myself from grabbing, touching, scratching anywhere and everywhere that I could. Tork took this new development in stride.

He pressed his hips into mine, our heavy cocks brushing past each other in the most delicious kind of friction. The way he rocked back and forth against me sent spark after spark of adrenaline, endorphins, and white-hot desire crackling across every vein, every pore, until I was no longer myself. I was his.

"Need to feel you," I whimpered, arching my back to grind against him again. "Inside me."

Tork rumbled low in his chest and dipped a hand below to test my opening. When he brought it back, his fingers were wet and covered with slick. "Looks like someone's quite excited," he teased and brought the fingers up to my mouth. I sucked them between my lips, licking him clean of my juices. It was so wrong, so embarrassing, so personal...

But so. Fucking. Hot.

"Please," I whispered, my voice breaking. My wild, half-lidded eyes met his, and in that moment our dragons sensed one another, soaring together and beginning their primal dance.

Tork stuck his hands under my buttocks and lifted my hips, putting my legs over his shoulders. I was so vulnerable, so exposed to him like this. But I'd have it no other way.

He slid into me without warning, the hot, hard length stretching and filling me completely. It wasn't long until he was seated all the way to the hilt, so deep inside me it pressed upon a secret place that came alive with the added pressure.

I moaned and rocked toward him again. Why wasn't he moving? Why wasn't he pounding me yet?

"A pounding, you say?" Tork teased me.

My face grew bright red, burning with the realization I'd said that to him in our minds. I had to learn how to split out my regular thoughts versus what I transmitted over our Link. I bit my lip and nodded. "Yes," I got out, but no other words would come.

"Hold on tight, baby." Tork gripped my hips and drew out of me, plunging back in so deeply and so suddenly that I cried out, my head arcing backward.

"Like that?" He asked, doing it again as if to demonstrate.

"Ah...Goddess...yes!" I could barely breathe, much less get out the words I needed as he dove into my channel again and again, stretching me beyond what I thought was possible and hitting that delicate spot each and every time. The tension drove higher still and my hand found my way to my own cock, pumping it in time with Tork's thrusts.

We rode together on a sea of sensation, each movement sending us higher and higher until...

"Goddess! Tork! Yes!" I spasmed around him as my release came, shattering and hard, echoing through every part of my body and spewing out of my cock in long white ropes. The mere sight of my pleasure took Tork over the edge with me, and he let my legs down to hold me, skin to skin, while he cried out and pumped into me, filling me with his seed.

It didn't matter that he was my father's best friend. It didn't matter that he was nearly twice my age. It didn't matter what people would say.

Let them talk. We were mates, fated by Glendaria herself. And as I came down from the heights of ultimate pleasure, I realized I wouldn't have had it any other way.

9

TORK

Another night, another bout of insomnia. I laid awake in bed next to Ansel, staring at the ceiling. No matter what I tried, my mind just wouldn't shut up.

I sighed and gently pulled myself out of bed, being careful not to disturb Ansel. I needed a drink of water, and I needed to think.

Just as soon as I'd poured myself a glass I heard a knock at the door. A soft, tentative knock, as if they weren't sure whether they should be here or not.

When I went to the door, I saw Lucien standing there, wearing a robe and holding a steaming mug in his hands.

"I figured you'd be up," he said softly. "Come, let's talk."

I glanced back at Ansel, still sleeping peacefully. "Okay, but make it quick." If he woke up and I wasn't there, I would never hear the end of it.

We walked through the alleyway with our drinks in hand, stepping over the loose cobblestones and taking in the silence of the night. Darkvale served as such a hub of activity during the day. But in the dead of night? It was like a graveyard.

"How is Alec doing in light of all this?" I asked after taking another sip of water. "With the Steamshire reveal and all."

"He's scared," Lucien said without missing a beat. "He's angry. We all are."

I stepped over a tree root that had bulged out of the ground and continued. "Do you think he could get through to them? The humans, I mean. They're from his village. Perhaps he could get them to see reason."

Lucien shrugged. "He couldn't before. That's why we got him and most of the kids and omegas out of there. Don't see why this time would be any different."

"Hmm," I groaned. He had a point. "I'm ready to fight with you," I blurted out. It was the only thing I could think to say in the moment, and that's what this was all leading to, wasn't it? Another battle. Another war. Would it ever end?

"I only wish it didn't have to come to that," Lucien said softly, kicking at a stone. He shook his head and changed the subject. "How's he doing?"

"Who, Ansel?" I took another sip of my water before responding. Even though just about everyone knew we were mates by now, it was still a little awkward to talk about. "He's fine. Tired, is all. The hormones are getting to him."

Lucien nodded knowingly. We came to a clearing lined with stone pillars, a vine covered trellis, and two great stone benches. We sat, listening to the high pitched whine of the wind.

"I remember when Alec was pregnant," he said with a smile. "There was nothing I wouldn't do to make sure he was comfortable and safe. Omegas aren't the only ones that change during pregnancy. I ran from our greatest battle to rescue him, remember?"

I nodded, remembering the day we took back our home. Remembering how Lucien rushed off in an instant and left Marlowe in charge.

"I remember."

"You know, a lot of people gave me weird looks for mating a human. I'm sure you'll get some of the same for your pairing. But I want you to know that you have my support. You two are perfect together."

I smiled and reflected on his words as a lightness filled me. It burned through my heart like honey, like a warm drink on the coldest winter's day. How grateful I was to have someone so special in my life!

"I guess I never let myself think of him that way, before." I shrugged and remembered the first time I'd seen him after he returned from the Academy. I'd noticed him. My dragon noticed him, too. But I hadn't thought anything of it, until that fateful night... "After the ball, I couldn't stop thinking about him. Hell, I didn't even know it *was* him back then. Just that something really big had happened, and I didn't know how to feel."

Lucien let out a hearty laugh at that, placing his hand over his belly. I hissed at him to quiet down, but we were surrounded by only trees. No homes nearby.

"Sounds like someone had a good time after all. Aren't you glad I dragged you along? Mr. 'Grr, I'm not going even if I have to wear a paper bag on my head'!" He kept laughing, and I grumbled.

"Whatever." I rolled my eyes, but could stop the laughter from bubbling up in my throat. It was kinda ridiculous, actually. So we laughed, letting go of all fear about the future, all tension, all stress of constant battle and paranoia. This was nice.

But nice things, shoulda known, never last.

Our reverie shattered as a whining alarm cut through the night. It chilled me right to my bones as the klaxon wailed and I leapt to my feet.

"What's going on?" Lucien cried over the din. He covered his ears and peered up at the sky, where the sound seemed to come from nowhere and everywhere at once. My thoughts instantly went to Ansel. He was alone. I had to get to him.

Stay right there, I warned him on our Link as I took off at a run. *I'm coming to get you!*

Lucien's footsteps pattered not far behind.

"The wards!" I shouted back at him. "Something's wrong, something's set them off—"

Just then a great shattering sound shook the earth. I nearly lost my footing and Lucien just about did, grabbing on to my sleeve as he swayed to the side. Electric arcs like lightning flashed through the sky as the magical dome protecting Darkvale disintegrated. A huge gaping hole yawned open in the force field and grew wider, like a mouth determined to eat everything in its path.

"You know how to fix it?" Lucien barked, staring up at the breach.

"I could try, but—"

"I can." We stopped short as Ansel appeared at the

door of my house, fully alert and suited up in his work clothes. He cracked his knuckles. "Sounds like you need a wardsman."

My heart and dragon soared when I saw him like this. Even though he wasn't feeling well, even though his hormones were going crazy, he was always ready to step up and defend his friends, family, and clan. Just one of many things I admired about him.

I regarded him with a wide, growing grin. "Yes. Yes, we do."

"Cover me," Ansel commanded, slinging his bag of tools over his shoulder. "I'm going in."

As the alarms roared above us and confused villagers began to emerge from their homes, Ansel ran off straight for the source of the danger. And even though part of me was terrified for his safety, another part had never been so proud in my life.

10

ANSEL

I fled through the chaos, my bag bumping against my leg as I set my sights on the control room housing most of the machinery for the wards. Part of my duty in Darkvale was to perform regular maintenance and updates, but since going on the road I hadn't had a chance to check on them again.

Good thing I was here, I thought in a flash as I ran. *What if the dome went down while I was away? Or worse*, I gulped, *if something happened to me?*

I made a mental note then and there to start training an underling of my own, so we'd have back up on the wards once I had the baby. My heart thudded faster at the thought.

That's right. I was having a baby. Two babies, actually. And I would protect them with everything I had.

I skidded to a stop in front of the control room and wrenched open the door, the warm, dry air of exhaust hitting me full in the face. I sputtered and dived in, squinting through the dim light to get to the control panel.

The ground shook again with the force of another blast. I fell against the wall with a yelp, the doorknob poking into my ribs. It stopped nearly as soon as it started, though, and I threw myself back into action. The control panel was locked for security reasons, but in the moment it was proving to be quite the inconvenience. I dug into every pocket for the key and turned up empty. Where was it? I finally found it at the bottom of my bag and yanked it out, my shaking hands only barely managing to get it into the keyhole before the ground shifted beneath me once more.

I threw open the panel and the scene that looked back at me couldn't have been much worse. The wards were fried, like some kind of electrical surge had come through and burned the lot of them out. We had override switches in place for just such a contingency—things sometimes went haywire during storms—but they weren't so easy to activate. You had to really get into the mechanics of it and align the resonance of the existing wards to the override. Not an easy task at the best of times, and when the world was crumbling around you? Even less so.

"Who designed this crap?" I grumbled to myself as I pulled out my screwdriver and slipped magnifying goggles over my face.

Oh right. Me.

Thanks a lot, asshole.

I poked around the bits of frayed wire, trying to feel through the metal to the resonance of magic within. That was the core of all magitech, after all. Imbuing a machine with one's essence allowed the engineer to create all sorts of improvements or abilities. But only if the correct resonance frequency was applied. Anything else, and the magic would backfire, causing a very messy, and very dangerous, result.

Sweat beaded up on my forehead as I let out a slow, shaky breath to still my hands. There were six switches marked in red that would turn on the backup wards, but to do that, I had to imbue them first.

Here goes nothing.

I reached out beyond the metal, deep down into my soul and the well of energy there. I listened for the calm, steady hum of the machine, almost like a beating heart. Each machine had a differing frequency that, when matched, upgraded the whole system. I tried to match what I heard, slowly letting go of a little bit of magic at a time, but it wasn't right.

The metal grew hot beneath my hands and I jerked my wrist back as a white shiny burn shone on my finger. I hissed and sucked it into my mouth, narrowing my eyes. *Come on, Ansel. Come on, they're counting on you.*

As if in response I felt an almost imperceptible pressure against my stomach, sorta like a gas bubble but stronger. I placed a hand over my swelling navel, wiping the sweat from my brow.

"Daddy's here," I soothed them, and prayed that I wouldn't let my babies down. One false move in here and I'd be blown to kingdom come, along with anyone unfortunate enough to be standing nearby.

A ripping sound echoed through the air and a panicked glimpse toward the small slatted window told me the rift was widening.

Dammit!

No matter what I tried, how deep I reached or how much I focused, I couldn't seem to get it right. I needed more. And I knew just where I might get that.

Tork, I called out on our Link. *Get your ass over here.*

What? The response came almost instantly. *What's wrong?*

Now!

My heart thudded in my chest as I groped out for the right resonance. Every time I started to grasp the elusive pattern, it slipped through my fingers like sand. I grit my teeth and tried again and again, watching in horror.

This didn't make any sense. I knew all the wards here in Darkvale. Built most of them myself, and yet this one continued to elude me. Any other time, it would have been routine, but not today. Stress? Hormones? Everything else that had been on my mind recently? No way to tell. I remembered the amp in power I'd felt when working with Tork. I remembered how every muscle lit up with strength and purpose, and I felt like I could move the world. To reinstate the wards after such a massive blowout, we were gonna need power. And a lot of it.

A scraping sound caught my attention and I whirled around, my hand on my weapon.

It's me, you bonehead, Tork's voice came from the other side of the door. *Open up.*

I let out a breath and let him in. Before I knew it he was on me, his arms wrapped around my waist and his face nuzzled in my neck. Already the humming, tingling flow of energy flowed from him to me, and back again like a live circuit.

Perfect.

"What's the crisis?" He asked, drawing back to look me in the eye.

"I need your help." I said, pointing to the control panel.

"With the wards?" Tork cocked an eyebrow. "Can't say it's my specialty, but..."

"No," I insisted and held him back. He watched me silently, waiting for my next move. "Listen to me and do exactly as I say. Take my hand."

Tork covered my hand with his own large and well-weathered one. He gave it a quick squeeze, sending blood to all the wrong places when I needed it to think.

"Feel that?" I asked breathlessly. My cock twitched in my pants. My dragon pouted in my chest.

One track mind, that one.

"Yeah," Tork rumbled, his breath hot against my ear.

"Now focus," I commanded as I moved back toward the control panel and began the ritual once more. "I'm gonna need all the juice we can get."

The world faded away as I tapped into the energy source coming across our Link, using it to refine the pattern in my mind, chipping away the rough edges until it matched that I saw in the machine exactly.

I gave his hand a squeeze and called upon my powers once more, pushing that energy into the metal. It flowed around each of the six wards like water, covering every crack and crevice. Then they started to heat up again, but the indicator lights still hadn't come on.

Something was still wrong.

"Come on, come on, come on," I muttered to myself as I screwed up my eyes, squinted through the metal to what I knew intuitively lie beneath. The energy that poured out of us reached around the core, but couldn't quite touch it. Like a badly copied key, the resonance was still not quite right.

The twins shifted in my belly once more and this time I felt a third surge of energy, small but definitely there. It flowed up into me from my center, reaching down my arms toward the tips of my fingers and out into the world.

Tork shivered and didn't let go. "Looks like they're getting into it too."

"Yeah," I breathed, and this time I knew it would work. It had to.

I reached out like before, but the energy came easier now. It wasn't like trying to jam a key into a rusty lock, but a gentler, smoother motion. It flowed in and around each of the wards in turn and I held my breath as the bright white indicator lights clicked on, one by one.

Six backup wards operational.

"Flip the switches," Tork said without taking his hand from mine.

Click. Click. Click. Click. Click. Click.

The mechanical whirring started again. The wards glowed white then green as they came online, and the wires crisscrossed themselves out of the control box down underground where they would, hopefully, restart the shield protocol.

The ground stabilized. The tearing sound stopped. I dared to throw open the door and peek out at the aftermath.

Healing over like a bad scar, tendrils of white light pressed up over the wound and across it, healing the part that had faltered. The air shimmered as the sun rose on the horizon, then with a flash of light the dome became whole once more.

"Woo!" I yelled, pumping my fist at the sky. Tork stood beside me and hollered his own triumph. He lifted our hands, still entwined, to the sky.

"We did it," I said, my shoulders slumping as the adrenaline began to wear off. "We're safe."

"You did it," Tork reminded me, and kissed my forehead. "My little engineer."

I blushed. I pressed my face into his chest and breathed in his scent. So good. "Thank you," I muttered without moving. It came out as no more than a mumble through the fabric of his shirt.

Tork grasped both sides of my face and tilted my head up to look at him. I grinned and gazed deep into those amber eyes, eyes that I could spend a lifetime admiring.

"I love you," Tork said, and then he kissed me.

11
———
ANSEL

After the shield crisis, things calmed down considerably around Darkvale. Well, calm for us. It had been almost two whole weeks without any life-threatening disasters!

I counted that as a win in my book.

The rest of the team had arrived from the field, bringing a wagon full of artifacts with them. Tork, of course, wanted to start delving into them immediately and holed up in the lab at just about all hours. I would have been helping him too, but I had other matters to attend to.

After the debacle with the shields, I realized we were going to need a more robust system if it ever came time for a real full-scale assault. The metal man we'd encountered still plagued my nightmares, and I'd be damned if they were getting through our shields.

I spent my days strengthening the wards and redesigning the override system. Of course, the work was a lot of stop and go. The twins were growing rapidly now, and I was constantly waylaid by bathroom breaks or sore joints. Dragon pregnancies were notoriously short, everyone knew that, but it was still early days. The fact that there was not one, but two babies inside me made everything feel twice as intense.

In just a few months time, I'd be a father. Tork and I both. The thought sent a chill down my spine. I had no idea how to be a father. No one ever taught me this stuff. How the hell was I going to take care of two babies at once?

Sure, I'd always thought about being a father. All omegas did, I figured. It was part of our DNA. But all that talk about mates and babies and knotting and heats was just that—talk. It sat peacefully in the back of my mind as something that happened to other people. Not to me.

Now that I was pregnant, it was like a whole new world of possibilities opened up for me. Things I hadn't considered before.

Perhaps having a baby was like the biggest science experiment of them all. I huffed in amusement at that realization, cupping my stomach with my free hand. I crafted all manner of magical and mechanical things in the lab. Things no one had ever thought of before. Things people thought were impossible. But this? This would be my greatest achievement: creating new life.

I drew in a slow steady breath through my nose and then let it out through my mouth, counting the seconds that passed. *In....out.* It was one of the first techniques Tork taught me when he became my mentor. Right after my dad died, my emotions, my mind, they were all a wreck. He helped me then, to put me back together before we started working. And those simple techniques? That kindness he'd shown me back then?

I still used them today.

I let out one more long, slow breath and stretched my shoulders, taking off my work apron for the day and discarding my gloves on the lab table.

Another day's work done.

Tork let me know on our Link he'd be working late, so I headed to dinner alone. As soon as I sat down Nikolas found me.

"Mind if we sit?" He asked. He bounced baby Hope on his hip and his five-year-old daughter Lyria stood beside him, balancing a plate of food.

"Go ahead, Tork's skipping dinner again." I rolled my

eyes. "He gets way into stuff sometimes, and all those artifacts the team brought back are no exception. I figure I'll take him a plate later."

"Good man." Nikolas got everyone settled and then turned to me, looking me up and down.

"How are you doing with everything? Marlowe told me how brave you were out there."

I looked away, my cheeks suddenly burning. "It's nothing."

"So you and Tork, huh?" He continued. "Can't say I'm surprised. I saw the way you looked when we dragged him out of that tunnel."

I snorted. "That obvious?"

"Totally."

"You don't think its, I dunno, weird?"

Nikolas clapped me on the back. "Look man. I fell for my best friend. Lucien fell for a human. We're all a little weird around here."

"How's Hope doing? Keeping you busy?"

Nik hoisted her. "Unbelievably. Her and Lyria both."

"I'm five years old now!" Lyria grinned at me, holding out five tiny fingers.

"Her birthday was just last week," Nik said while

spooning some baby food to little Hope. Gotta say, the ability of parents to multi task was impressive. "She's starting school soon. Thomas won't know what hit him."

I watched the little family eat together, Lyria chewing on a roll while Nik fed Hope what looked like creamed peas. They looked just like him and Marlowe, perfect little renditions of the both of them. They made for adorable children, and even fiercer dragons, I was sure. My heart filled with gratitude and wonder as I watched them interact. What must that be like, having children? Having a family to love and care for?

One day soon, I'd have that too.

Our own little family.

"Hey," Nik said and shook me out of my thoughts. "You need anyone to talk to about...I dunno, anything, you come to me, okay? I got your back."

I had a mate. I had friends. I had a clan that supported and surrounded me. And soon, two tiny baby dragons.

"Thanks man." I nodded. "I appreciate it."

"What are friends for?" Nik wiped a smear of peas from Hope's cheek and looked back at me. His voice dropped and he leaned closer as if he was about to share a secret. "Oh, and tell Tork not to freak out too much. Alphas, man. they get so wrapped up when we're pregnant, don't they? Can't help themselves."

That got a full on laugh out of me. My shoulders shook. "You got that right." My mind drifted to the way he always double checked to make sure I had everything I needed before going to bed at night. The way he'd bend over backwards to get whatever I was craving, no matter how weird it was. "He's been great."

"That means he's a keeper. Where is he tonight, anyway?"

"Couldn't make it," I said after a spoonful of hot stew that burned my throat as it went down. Myrony had really outdone herself this time. Carrots, celery, and potatoes floated in a beef broth rich with salt and spices. "He's been working day and night on the prototypes Rex brought back from the field. He keeps saying he's close to a breakthrough, but..." I shrugged.

"Typical Tork."

"He's passionate," I said after another spoonful of soup. *In more ways than one.*

Hope made a wet coughing sound and green goop spewed out of her mouth, dribbling down the sides of her face and dripping onto Nik's clothes. He grimaced and held her at arms length, but his expression was still every bit the loving father. I offered him a towel to clean up with, but he brushed it away.

"Looks like that's my cue," he said, untangling himself from the long communal bench. "Bedtime comes early, anyway." He balanced Hope on his hip and waved to me with his free hand. "It was great to see you again."

"Take care!" I waved at him as they headed off back toward their home.

The pregnancy hormones were definitely having their way with me now. Did I just find a puking baby cute?

Tork would never let me hear the end of that.

Tork.

The thought sliced across my mind like a knife. No, a hot knife, being struck by lightning. My dragon cried out in pain and spikes of terror raced across my flesh. My hand shot to my temple.

Something was wrong. Something was happening to Tork!

My vision faded in and out, leaving me seeing double for a few seconds as I shook my head and blinked my eyes. What was going on? Where was he? I tried to call out to Tork on our Link but got no answer. Only cold, empty static.

Ice water dumped into my belly and my skin broke out in gooseflesh as my dragon cried out once more.

Find him! Find him now!

I nearly knocked over the table as I ran toward the lab, terrified of what I might find. *Tork, answer me! Tork, it's Ansel. Are you okay?* I called out to him again and again in my mind, hoping that perhaps he was just too far or was too entranced in his work to notice. But no, there was no answer. And that worried me even more.

I fumbled with my keycard and threw open the door to the laboratory, only to find it cold, dark, and empty.

Tork was gone.

12

TORK

The sun sank low over the horizon and cast a warm red glare over everything. The hot fumes of the workshop broke out in sweat over my skin, not to mention the way the mask over my face recirculated the same stale air again and again.

But I couldn't stop yet. I had to figure this out.

Ever since Rex had brought back a wagon full of mysterious artifacts from our scouting journey, I was obsessed. There was mostly scrap metal and other assorted traveling supplies, but some very interesting pieces as well that I'd never seen before. A little voice in the back of my head kept telling me that if I kept working, kept pushing, I could find that hidden key to turn the tides in our favor.

As of yet, I hadn't found it.

I wiped my brow and moved on to the next item, an ornately carved mirror framed with ivory and perfectly reflective, even after the dusty journey. It was far too nice a piece of work to be carrying in a travel wagon. Looked like it would be on display at the Flower Festival or in a merchant's cart, not some roving band on the road.

I flipped it over and examined the backside. Smooth, cream colored ivory encircled the glass and shone in the light. I rubbed the pads of my fingers over the surface and closed my eyes.

There.

I couldn't quite tell what it was, but there was some form of engraving on the back. I could feel it, but no matter how I tilted the mirror I couldn't get it to come to light. Finally I moved to the wood-powered forge and grabbed one of the blocks there. I shoved it into the furnace and charred only the end, then rushed back to my work.

Using the firewood like a giant pencil I scraped it over the pristine ivory, throwing crumbs of wood and black dust everywhere. It ran over the fine engraving and the charcoal dust stuck into the grooves. Now each letter stood out plain as day. I wiped away the dust with a smear of my hand and there it was: the inscription.

It didn't look like any language I'd seen before, though I wasn't a linguistic expert like some of the other engineers. I mostly just blew shit up. Something about this mirror gave off an eerie presence though. Like it was some precious, mystical artifact I should never have picked up in the first place.

I mouthed the words scratched in to the back of the ivory.

~ Andelra intimi laosin acree ~

Beneath it was a scratched insignia of six points in a hexagon shape connected through by lines. I furrowed my brow as I studied the strange markings. What did it mean?

That's when the mirror started vibrating in my hands.

I nearly dropped it in my surprise, but that would have broken the glass. Then whatever knowledge this thing had would be lost. Thoughts flashed briefly in my mind of putting this off till later, of recruiting someone that knew more about this kind of stuff than I did. but I was in too deep now. I had to keep going.

I flipped over the mirror, the ivory and glass still buzzing beneath my fingertips. Only this time, when I peered into the smooth glass surface, I didn't see my face staring back at me. It was like looking through a portal. Or a window, maybe. Green hills rolled across the landscape and clouds drifted lazily by in the skies above. It looked sorta familiar, like I'd been there before. Nearby, if I had to guess.

Then they crested the hill and my heart froze in my chest.

Not one mech. Not two.

Five of them. Five fully operational, totally badass automatons, controlled by the humans of Steamshire and rumbling across the way. That's when I realized where they were. That was not half a day from here. That was part of the ground we'd covered not too long ago.

They were coming. They were coming for Darkvale. And they were close.

I couldn't tear my eyes away as I watched all five of them creaking and rumbling and tearing up the ground in their wake. This was bad. No, this was more than bad.

This was a disaster.

Lucien had reached out for aid for but as far as I knew, they weren't coming. At least not in time to save us, anyway. Guess we were gonna have to go this alone.

We'd protect our home, or go down trying.

My dragon did a panicked dance in my chest, begging to come out and roast anyone or anything that stood in our way. I had more than just myself to live for now. I had a mate. And not only that, my mate was pregnant, with twins of all things.

They wouldn't get to my family. I'd die before I let that happen.

The emotion surged through me and blocked out all reason. I had to protect him. No matter what.

I looked across the lab table to the work area where I'd been building a new type of explosive mine. Using what I had learned about the automatons, I had specifically engineered a new prototype to take them down before they ever neared our walls.

Five mines lay on the table.

Five automatons approached our walls.

I chewed my lip. They weren't quite ready yet, was the problem. There were still a few bugs I needed to work out, like the one where the trigger mechanism occasionally didn't stay locked. I could arm the mine, walk away, and it would switch off on its own without warning. A lot of good that did.

But it was this or nothing.

The mirror clattered to the desk as I made up my mind. I took a deep breath, stuffed the mines in my bag, and flew out the door. As soon as I breached the castle gates, I gave myself over to the shift.

Dragon time.

———

I flew faster than I'd ever flown in my life, the bag at my side dangling precariously as I flapped my wings faster, harder. Wind wailed in my ears and my eyes watered. But the heart of a warrior beat within me, the heart of an alpha, a mate, a father. *Protect your clan. Protect your family,* it told me. My dragon was on a mission, and it would not be deterred.

I landed on the grass right over the hill that shielded Darkvale on one side. I couldn't see them yet, but the echoes I heard in the distance told me they wouldn't be far. My fingers fumbled on the switches as I placed each of the five mines and used the mounting spike I'd developed to bury them into the earth. They weren't going anywhere. And once the automatons ran over them, neither would they.

My brain reminded me that this was crazy. That I was breaking just about every clan law and I should have gone to Lucien first, to warn him. And I would have, really, had things been different.

There was no time.

By the time I'd alerted all the proper authorities and gathered a team to help head them off, they'd be upon us, and we'd be toast. But if I could set up this first line of defense, if I could blast my way through their defenses before they even got close to the walls...

Maybe we'd have a chance.

Glendaria preserve us, I muttered in an incantation, crossing my hands over my heart.

I armed each of the mines one by one, holding my breath as a little red light flashed on the side then faded away. Now as long as they didn't malfunction and trigger early, or turn themselves off like my early prototypes had...

When I flipped the switch on the last mine, it came off in my hand and the mine blinked an angry red, flashing its warnings at me. I sucked in a breath. Two choices spread out before me:

I could stay here and manually configure the last mine.

Or I could run and hope it didn't blow before I got out of range.

Both of them, I realized grimly, likely ended in a fiery death. Mine, to be exact.

I'm sorry, I thought through my Link, praying that

Ansel would be able to hear me. *I'm sorry and I love you.*

Then I held tight to the mine, suppressing the trigger, and roared out my defiance into the night.

If I was gonna go out, I'd go out with a boom.

13

ANSEL

I heard Tork's plea at the same time the alarms started going off.

I'm sorry and I love you.

What kind of crazy scheme was he up to this time?

My heart cried out in protest and I nearly shifted right there in the middle of the lab in my haste to get to him.

Sirens wailed and I heard Lucien's voice, amplified one hundred times as he announced that the final battle was at hand. He called us to arms, not only the alphas, but omegas, women, everyone who could fight. Especially without reinforcements, we needed every fighting hand we could get.

I rushed through the chaos and into the throng of shifters pushing their way through the gates. Marlowe led the vanguard, his eyes fierce and furious as he beckoned to his strongest fighters. They shifted as soon as they were clear of the gates and sailed high into the sky, encircling the fortress with a moat of flame.

I escaped the ring of fire just in time, grateful for my small stature.

That's when I saw him.

Our eyes met and time stopped for a split second as I realized his predicament.

Ansel, no! He screamed in my mind, but I was already running toward him.

If you touch me, you'll trigger it! We'll both blow!

No we won't!

I wouldn't let that happen. Not to my mate, not to my babies, not to anyone. This time, I could be a savior.

A wall of metal crested the hill and turned my blood to ice. So that's what all the alarms were about. So that meant they were coming. They were here. I eyed the line of explosives and realized that Tork had snuck out to do this on his own, before any of us even knew they were coming.

He wanted to protect me.

But now it was time to protect him.

I grit my teeth and threw myself into the shift, my wings sprouting from my back just in time. I swooped forward and never took my eyes off Tork, who looked on with fear, surprise, and what I thought could have been admiration.

Energy and adrenaline pumped through me and my heart hammered like a drum even in my dragon form as the wind rushed against my scales. I hovered low, reaching out my strong back legs and stretching the claws there. If I could just grab him in time, we could get out of here and away from the blast.

And if I messed up, I'd both impale my mate and get blown up at the same time.

No pressure.

I sucked in a breath and locked my sights on my mate.

Too late, he realized what I was doing and put his hands up to shield his face. My legs reached down and caught him around the middle, careful of my talons. Tork yelped as he flew into the air with me and as we sailed away from the scene, the malfunctioning mine exploded in our wake. Fire and heat burned at my back but I couldn't stop. I pushed my wings harder, up and away.

Let me down! Goddess please, let me down! Tork screeched from below me, still wriggling in my grasp.

Oh, thank Glendaria. He was alive.

I flew in a wide circle over the plains, past the encroaching automatons and over the wall of flame protecting Darkvale. I landed as gently as I could and Tork tumbled out of my grasp, rolling a few times before coming to a stop, dusty and scraped up, on the ground. He stared at me, open mouthed, brushing his torn clothes off with skinned hands while he fought to catch his breath. I watched every move.

Fucking hell, Ansel. Tork grumbled on our Link. *Warn a guy next time!*

You were about to die, I shot back. *I'm supposed to let you sacrifice yourself like that?*

*Just...*he shuddered. *Never do that again.*

Stubborn, I teased. *I saved your ass.*

Reckless, he muttered.

My dragon huffed. He was one to talk.

I changed back to human form, my limbs already exhausted from my frenzied rescue. Tork ran forward and threw his arms around me, squeezing me so tightly I couldn't breathe.

"I get it, I get it," I squeaked and pushed him away.

"If something happened to you..." he said out loud this time. "You scared me, Ansel."

"Ready for a little more of that teamwork magic?" I asked him as I took his hand. The power of our ancestors flowed through us and strengthened my will, my resolve, and my courage. All past hurts and fears fled away in the presence of my mate and the growing life within me.

"Let's do this," Tork agreed and kissed me on the cheek. "Dragon style."

In that moment no one else mattered. Our dragons united, our bodies and minds totally in sync. We shifted in unison, and took to the skies.

———

We sailed over the front lines, watching as man and dragon converged on the battlefield.

Marlowe and his team circled above with fire and fury, but what surprised me most of all were the forces on the ground.

None other than Alec Cipher led a team of omegas into the fray, shouting war cries to the heavens and pumping his fist to the sky. They followed him. They believed in him.

And his band of freedom fighters weren't just shifters, either. There were humans there, too. Former Steamshire refugees. With Steamshire insurgents clattering over the hill in their massive metal men, it would be a sight to behold.

I had always known that humans and shifters didn't like one another very much. But to stoop to this level...it chilled me to the core. And here they were, in their own little civil war, right at our doorstep. Because this was more than just a fight over land or property. This was a fight of ideals, and the victor would pave the way for the future of their species. Humans and shifters had learned to work together in Darkvale because of Alec and Lucien's firm belief that we could live as one.

But if Steamshire were to win today? I shuddered to think.

"For Darkvale!" I roared and let out a jet of flame. We would never go back. Never.

The automatons continued to roll forward, the weapons built into their hulking hands quivering at the ready.

When they hit the mines, we blast 'em, Tork said in my mind. *I'll take the west flank. You take the other.*

Deal.

We split off and came up on them from either side, drawing their attention away from the oncoming army. One raised its arm and shot a bolt toward me. I swerved to the side just in time. Tork barrel rolled through the air and picked up speed, dodging in and out of their attacks.

Three... Tork breathed.

Two, I joined in.

One.

"Boom," I mouthed.

The mines exploded on impact and created a wall of debris as metal and dirt flew everywhere. I didn't waste any time unleashing my fire, spraying death down upon the wreckage. I couldn't see through the smoke and ash, I couldn't hear over the deafening sounds of the explosion, but I continued breathing fire with all my heart, and Tork's too.

This went past any limit I'd set for myself before. I was putting my all into this and then some more. As the fire dried up and sparks coughed up and I heaved for breath, I prayed to the Goddess above it was enough. That when the dust cleared and the smoke settled, those awful things would be dead.

No such luck.

Through the fire and explosions of the mines, four out of the five automatons still stood. Still advanced. My stomach heaved, another wave of nausea seizing me like a snake. This time it wasn't morning sickness. This time it was the crippling, crushing realization that despite our best efforts, we'd failed.

Fall back! Tork called to me, and I didn't waste any time.

We sailed over the crowd of humans and shifters pouring from the gate, and I shifted back into human form to join them.

"We've weakened them," I called out to Alec as soon as I touched down. "But they're still coming. You're gonna need to give it everything you've got."

"You hear that?" Alec projected to the crowd around him. "Today is the day we fight! Not only for our home, not only for our safety, but for our freedom! It does not matter, brothers and sisters, what land you hail from, what species or race you are, what powers you have or don't have. What matters is our drive, our dedication, our love for one another and for our family. I know many of you are refugees, just as I once was. It saddens my heart to see the Elders have done this. But each and every one of you means more to me than a thousand Elders and their schemes. Today we fight! Today we win! Will you join me, Darkvale?"

The crowd roared, brandishing whatever weapons they had on hand.

Dragons shifted and roars crackled through the air like

lightning. It was now or never, and I'd never been so proud of my clan.

Just then, the mechs slashed through the flames, stepping through as if they were nothing. My throat closed up in horror. The mines hadn't worked. Fire hadn't worked. How were we gonna take these bastards down?

One of the automatons spoke for the first time, amplifying his own voice as him and his cronies moved ever closer.

"Alec Cipher...it's no wonder I should find you here. Still dwelling with the animals, I see. And got a whole army of traitors with you too. How...quaint."

Alec bared his teeth and I wanted to blast the metal man right then and there.

"You've gone too far." Alec stood his ground and gestured to the fighters around him. "We don't subscribe to your ways of fear and hate anymore."

A moment of defiant, taunting laughter. "You brought an army of *omegas* against us? That's the best you can do?" The man laughed again, momentarily off his guard.

"Get them," Alec commanded.

A whole horde of men, women, and shifters surged forward like the tide, spilling over the ground and screaming their defiance as they faced off against their former masters. Dragons shifted and took to the air, flapping their wings in a swirling air current around the automatons.

The automatons stood ready, firing charges into the crowd. In unison they brought their feet up and then down in a mighty stomp, sending a shockwave through the earth. People stumbled and fell to their knees as the charges triggered and let out spurts of corrosive poison all over the onlookers. The mass of people soon devolved into chaos, humans shrieking and flailing as flesh sloughed away on impact of the ghastly green stuff from the charges.

It didn't stop everyone though. I ran forward with Adrian and Nik at my side, the three of us sharing a glance. Tork flew on scaly wings above us with Marlowe, leading the charge and pummeling into the mech firing the charges. They collided with a bone-jarring crash and and ear-splitting screech of metal and monster.

I set my sights on the rightmost mech and bared my teeth. This ended now.

Nik and Adrian flanked me and we converged on the monster, weapons at the ready. I gripped the gun I'd grabbed from the lab and took a deep breath. I hoped it would do what it said on the tin. Electromagnetic Pulse Detonation Device—Single Use, it read in silver engraving on the long polished barrel. My hands shook. I'd never fired a gun before, but here, in the presence of my kinfolk and all I held dear, there was no other option. I looked down the iron sights, lined up the pulsing heart of light at the mech's center, let out a breath, and pulled the trigger.

It hit the mech dead center like a load of invisible bricks. The metal man stumbled backwards and the throbbing ball of energy at its core flickered, faltered, and went out. The animated metal slumped and squealed, crashing to the dirt in a pile of dust.

"Woot!" Nik shouted, pumping his fist in the air. But as I kept my eyes on the now-unmoving automaton, I felt a chill of terror down to my very soul. This was wrong, this was very, very wrong. I stumbled back just in time.

The trapdoor holding the driver sprung open and a hooded man leapt out, eyes shining with supreme hatred and fury.

The driver wasn't a human at all.

It was a Sorcerer, and he didn't look happy.

14

TORK

We were in deep shit.

I knew Steamshire had Sorcerers on their side, sure, but to have them piloting these monsters?

My blood ran cold as I felt the clash of our energies in mid air. My throat dried up, my dragon quailed as I tumbled to the ground in human form. No shifting here.

I bared my teeth and clenched my fists.

"Sorcerer," I spat.

"Shifter," she responded, and when she let down her hood I saw with horror it was the same woman who'd escaped us.

Why had we ever let her escape? I bet the slippery

bitch told them all about us, too. That's why they withstood the mine blasts. That's why they kept coming through the wall of fire.

The echo of steel sounded behind me as my clansmen drew their swords. Sorcerer or not, they could still bleed. And they would pay for what they'd done here today.

"Grenya, is that you?" Heavy footsteps pushed through the crowd and I glanced over my shoulder long enough to see Elias striding toward the front lines.

Turns out we had a Sorcerer too.

"Elias..." The woman growled, narrowing her eyes. Her pale, glistening eyes tore straight through the crowd and chaos, straight to him. "How interesting to find you here. Thought you'd died."

"Far from it," Elias said. "Let's just say I turned over a new leaf."

"Traitor!" Grenya yelled so loud I took a few steps backward. "You've betrayed us all, Elias. Allying with these beasts? What were you thinking?"

"That we deserve more than a life of running from one job to the next."

"If your father could see you now..." Grenya's face twisted in disgust. "I should just get rid of you myself."

"Then come at me," Elias taunted. "But I'm not going anywhere."

I dodged out of the way just in time as their spells collided in midair.

A Sorcerer on Sorcerer battle? Not something you want to be caught in the middle of.

"Tork, come on!" Ansel's voice snapped me out of it. I joined him at his side and only then noticed the spent pistol in his hands. My pistol. It was nothing more than a hobby project I picked up on spare nights and weekends, yet Ansel had picked it up at just the right time to save us all.

"It worked!" I grinned, letting out a relieved laugh. "Awesome!"

"Celebrate later, we've got company!" He yanked me to the side just in time to miss a bolt flying through the air and burying itself, quivering, in the soft wet ground.

With a lump in my throat, I whirled around.

Those bastards!

While we'd been preoccupied the last remaining mech had snuck their way up to the gates, fighting now in close quarters with the omega army.

And we were losing.

Fear squeezed my heart like a vise. All those omegas,

fighting for their home and their freedom, some even younger than Ansel. The alpha instinct in me riled up and my dragon strained to break free, but the sorcerer was still too close, still doing her dirty work.

No matter. We had other means of fighting.

Ansel must have heard what I was saying, because he grabbed my hand and gave me a encouraging nod. I focused all my attention on the incoming mechs and charged forward, picking up a long spear from a fallen warrior as I went. I yelled and leapt into the air, aiming right for the gap between the monster's head and body.

The blade slipped into the gap in the metal and sent a shock of vibration from my hands all the way down my body. I cried out, hanging on to the spear for dear life as it lodged itself deeper into the machinery. There was a grinding, scraping sound and the mech wailed in a great rusty scream, flinching away so fast I nearly flew through the air with the force of it. I growled and held firm, driving it ever deeper, into the pulsing core and through the other side.

But when it flailed again and headed straight for my friend Adrian, I lost my grip and tumbled to the dirt.

No, Adrian...

No!

I skidded across the ground and held my breath, waiting for the screams.

"Don't mess with Darkvale!" A voice bellowed, and Adrian appeared on the other side, landing a roundhouse kick right at the weak part where the spear protruded. I let go at the last second and the spear snapped as the force split the mech in two, the pieces crashing to the ground in a smoking heap.

"The driver!" I cried to Adrian as I picked myself up. "Get the driver!"

By this time the driver's compartment had opened and a small, gangly man scrambled out, eyes frantic with fear. He held up his hands in surrender, but it was too late for that. Adrian and Alec grabbed him around the middle, holding him still while Ansel and I advanced.

I prepared to unleash a bout of flame but the sparks dried on my tongue and wouldn't come. Goddess-damned Sorcerer! I dared not look back, I dared not focus on anything but the present moment. The human screamed and tried to wriggle away, but was no match for his captors.

He didn't look so scary now, out of his giant metal contraption. He looked terrified.

Alec broke the silence before I had the chance to. "Why are you doing this, Hans?" His voice took on a pleading quality. He knew the man, I realized with a shock.

Hans sputtered and gulped, looking wildly at the battle raging around him. "I didn't have a choice, man. They made me..." He stopped, panting and coughing. "They made me a deal and I..."

"Denounce them and their ways," Alec commanded. "And you may yet live."

The man panted, eyes flickering between him and us. Fire still boiled in my gut, and I knew were I in Alec's shoes I would not have such mercy. These people had betrayed him, attacked him, killed members of their own tribe! There was no greater crime.

"Alec, you can't be serious—" I started, my own rage bubbling over. Ansel put a calming hand on my shoulder and I snapped my mouth shut.

"Lucien will deal with him," Alec sneered and passed him off to two burly-looking guards who dragged the screaming man away. Then he turned his gaze to me.

"You don't know what its like," he said softly, his voice wavering. "I lived with them for so long, and some of them were my friends, and..." He ran a hand over his face. "It's just hard to believe they're all bad, you know?"

I nodded and Ansel squeezed my hand.

A resounding boom echoed from behind us and my hands shot up to cover my ears, still pounding from the blast. I whirled around and found Elias standing over the rebel Sorcerer, his hand clenched in midair. Grenya gasped and clawed at her throat, her mouth opening and closing silently.

"You will not harm me and my friends anymore." He said it simply, as a statement of fact. Then he closed his outstretched hands into a fist, and the woman's eyes bulged and tongue sagged as her face turned a bright, beet red. She scrabbled at her neck until her arms went limp, sagging loosely by her side as her body gave up the fight. She was dead.

Elias stood over him for a long moment, considering the face of his enemy, a Sorcerer just like him. I knew how hard that must have been for him. When I first met Elias, he was a snarky little brat that wouldn't listen to anyone, least of all any Firefang. But he'd been such a resource to us as time went on. We'd developed a working relationship that perhaps was not close like friendship, but a solid trust and sharing of skills and ideals.

And this, here today? Elias had faced off against his own kind to protect us. He'd chosen a side at last. And he'd chosen us.

Elias turned, caught my eye, and bowed his head. "Kill them," I saw him mouth over the roar of battle.

Didn't have to tell me twice.

The roar of dragonfire filled the night as my people regained their powers. Men and women shifted all around me, taking to the sky and surrounding the remaining mech. Now that we knew their weakness, it was only a matter of time. The circling dragons built a towering prism of fire surrounding the mech and the ground armies stood on the other side, waiting to strike. I saw them dive-bombing from above, their claws outstretched, their wings folded to their side to pick up speed.

At the last second they leveled out, three dragons grabbing the mech in their claws and lifting it into the air. I heard screams now, human screams.

I watched with horror as they flew up, up, up, then split off in opposite directions while still holding the mech firmly in their claws. A great screech rent the air as debris tumbled to the ground. They had torn the mech limb from limb, and the driver along with it.

I tried not to think about the wet squish the body made as it hit the ground. I didn't think about the smell of soot or iron or smoke. In that moment, there was silence. Pure, blessed silence. The mechs were destroyed. Their masters incapacitated.

It was over.

Ansel leaned into me and let out a breath. He squeezed

his eyes shut, breath coming in quick gasps. I held him there in the middle of the battlefield, brushing a hand through his hair as the chaos died down around us.

After all the fear and blood and death, we'd done it. We'd won.

Over Steamshire and humans and Sorcerers, we'd come out on top.

I heard shouts and cheers of triumph behind us, but they faded into the background as I held my mate close. There was only one thing my dragon wanted to do right now, and we'd need a little more privacy for that.

15

ANSEL

fter the Battle of the Mechs, as we'd come to call it, things actually calmed down around Darkvale for once. We repaired, we recuperated, we recovered. Us Firefangs were nothing if not resilient.

Weeks passed as we fell into a sort of routine once more. We'd salvaged what we could from the wreckage of the automatons and brought it into the lab for testing and research. No one had been more excited about that than Tork, but we'd all had a hand in deciphering their technology.

After long nights of trial and error, combined with Elias' help, we'd managed to dissect the molten core that powered each automaton. It was such a marvelous source of energy, capable of more than just terror and destruction. In fact, I had an idea in my mind that we could make our own mechs in the future. Not for war, no. But for assistance. Several of our fighters had been injured, some even crippled in the attack. Add to that our elderly population and you had a contingent of people that could use a little help now and then.

All that had to be put on hold as I grew more and more pregnant, however.

The cravings were driving both me and Tork nuts, even though he didn't want to admit it. He was a good sport about it, though. He brought me pickles, ice cream, even a few rare berries. Whatever I asked for, he made it his mission to find. And that was only one of the reasons I loved him so much. As the days droned on though, I had to take leave from the lab because the little ones were not big fans of me standing around all day. My ankles swelled, my back ached.

I was ready for this to be over.

My stomach had ballooned out like I'd swallowed a watermelon whole, and even though Doctor Parley assured me everything was progressing smoothly, most days I felt like a beached whale.

It was only a week and a half before my due date when we received a formal message from Steamshire. Lucien gathered us all together in the great hall to read it aloud.

Steamshire had surrendered, at long last.

After years on the endless cycle of war and recovery, it felt weird to go about my daily schedule without waiting for the other shoe to drop. After I got used to it, it felt kinda...nice.

Clan Alpha Lucien announced a feast of epic proportions that weekend to celebrate our victory and to rekindle our spirits.

I was so there, of course. Only problem was all my fancy costumes wouldn't fit my over my belly. Believe me, I tried.

Tork, on the other hand? He was gonna take a little more convincing.

———

"Come on," I knocked on the bathroom door. "Come out already, you can't look that bad!"

I heard a muffled grunt from within and he finally emerged.

My mouth hung open as I took in this new Tork. Not only had he actually brushed his hair for once, he was wearing a suit. It hugged him in all the right places, accentuating his broad chest and the long lines of his legs.

"Like what you see?" He quirked a grin, turning around to give me a 360 view.

Damn, those pants were *made* for his ass.

"Oh, um," I rubbed the back of my neck and cleared my throat. "You look great. More than great, actually."

"Oh yeah?" He murmured, towering over me.

"Makes me wanna tear those clothes off right here." I grinned and dropped my voice. Even though no one else was around, it felt like our little secret.

"This is a brand new suit," Tork said in mock affront. "At least let me get through the dinner first."

I laughed. "You don't even want to go. We could stay here, you know...skip out..." I tried to give him a coy glance.

His eyes flashed with desire as he leaned in close, his hot breath whispering on my ear. "No, we're going. But after? After is fair game."

"Deal," I breathed. My dragon was already starting to get excited and a rush of heat down to my groin short-circuited what I wanted to say next. Waiting through the feast would be torture.

"The most delicious kind," Tork nipped at the side of my neck. Had I said that aloud? "But come on, let's get going."

He helped me to my feet—the babies made it hard nowadays—and we headed out the door to the ballroom. The very place where we'd ran into each other that fateful night.

———

The festivities were in full swing when we arrived. It wasn't as extravagant as the Flower Festival—but then, what was—but there was a colorful array of foods, live music, and every one of my friends was in attendance.

It was like a big family reunion. All of us, at last, were together. Were safe.

"You scout out a seat," Tork offered. "I'll grab us some food. What are the little ones craving today?"

I chewed my lip, thinking. "Pretzels? Or anything salty, really. And chocolate, if they have it."

Tork's face twisted into a grin. "Your wish is my command." He gave an exaggerated bow and headed off. I had to laugh.

"You've got him wrapped around your finger," I heard a voice from behind me as I watched him leave.

It was Adrian, one of the local omegas and a friend to Alec and Nik. I hadn't had a chance to get to know him very well since I was off at the Academy, but I'd heard great things.

I laughed again and shrugged. "Yeah, guess I do. He's just trying to help, is all."

"He's a good alpha. Takes care of his own." For a second his face sagged with something like sadness, or a long-forgotten memory. Then it was gone, as quickly as it had surfaced.

"He is," I agreed. "He's a keeper, for sure."

Adrian held a small one in his arms, but by the look of it he wouldn't be small much longer. Ink-black hair lay messily over his forehead and he gaped at me with wide amber eyes.

"This is little Finley," he said. "Say hi, Finley!"

The child buried his head in his daddy's shoulder instead. Adrian adjusted him on his hip and shrugged. "He's feeling shy tonight. Heard you have a little one of your own coming soon." He grinned and eyed my midsection. It wasn't exactly easy to hide anymore. My due date was still a week away, but I didn't know if I could wait that long. Pregnancy was awesome in a lot of ways, but I was ready to move on. I was ready to meet my little darlings and welcome them to the world.

"He's adorable," I cooed at the little one. I instinctively placed a hand over my stomach, thinking about my little ones on the way. "And yeah, you're right. Two, actually."

Adrian's eyes widened. "Twins? No way, man."

"Twins," I confirmed.

"Wow..." Adrian seemed at a loss for words. "They're incredibly rare, you know? I can't wait to meet them."

"Neither can I," I said, and my heart surged with pride.

"I don't envy all the work, though." Adrian said. "This little monster keeps me on my toes, but two? Sounds like a party."

I laughed. "I'm sure it will be." I wasn't as nervous about the birth as I probably should be. It was scary, sure. And having two babies to take care of instead of one was gonna be a lot of work. But I had faith that Tork and I could pull it off. When I was with him, anything seemed possible. Even raising twins.

Tork returned to the table with a plate full of food and set it before me. A big pile of pretzels, cured meat, and even a small wedge of chocolate. I stared at the plate and back at Tork. "Have I ever told you how much I love you?"

"Regularly." He sat down next to me and pecked my cheek. "But I never get tired of hearing it."

The moment was broken by the high pitched sound of silverware on glass. We all looked up to see Clan Alpha Lucien standing at the front of the room. He was joined by his mate Alec and their baby Corin. Nikolas and

Marlowe were there too with Lyria and Hope by their side.

The gang's all here, I thought with a smile.

"Greetings, Firefangs," Lucien said in a loud projecting voice. It reached across the room without amplification. He didn't need it. Everyone was still and listening. "Greetings to our friends and allies from Steamshire and abroad. We dine together tonight beyond the bounds of clans or races or labels. We dine together tonight as family. We've been through a lot in the past years. No one will deny that. But it is our commitment to our duty, and to each other, that has brought us here today. I say we toast to our friends, toast to our fallen comrades, and toast to all the bounty that is to come." He raised his glass high and the rest of us followed suit.

Alec spoke next. "The night I left Steamshire, I didn't know where I was gonna go, or what I was gonna do. I just knew I was destined for something greater than their ritual sacrifice. That night, I met Lucien. He took me in, showed me what a real family could be like. And what do you know? I fell in love. Dragons, shifters, sorcerers, humans, it doesn't matter. Alpha or omega, it doesn't matter. What we've built here is a model for the rest of the world, and I toast today to all the days to come, and all the new allies we'll meet along the way."

"Cheers," the crowd rumbled.

Nik now took the platform, raising his glass to the sky. "When I saw Darkvale burning around me, when I lost my mate that terrible night, I thought that's all life was. When I had my daughter and her alpha daddy wasn't there to see her beautiful smile, I kept moving. Even though I was treated no better than a hostage, I held that hope in my heart, night after night. *Firefangs mean family*. That's what Lucien told us. And when the Paradox finally fell, I knew my waiting had paid off. I not only re-united with my long lost mate, my best friend, my lover, but we had another perfect child together to add to our family. So my toast is to Hope— both the baby," he kissed his daughter's cheek—"and the concept that's brought us through so many trials to this day. To Hope!"

"To hope!" Voices echoed through the halls.

Marlowe was last, and he looked upon the crowd of friends and family, spreading his arms wide as if in a hug. "I'm not sure what I can say that hasn't already been said," he started. "I've fought with many of you throughout the years. I've worked with more. I've seen men and women, alphas and omegas, rise above their circumstances to greatness when called upon. And I have never been so proud to be surrounded with so many strong, caring, and generous people. So my toast is to strength—both the inner and outer strength that each and every one of you has inside. To strength!" He ended on a yell, jutting his glass into the air so quickly his drink splashed out.

"To strength!" The crowd echoed, and the air vibrated with the roars of dragons.

All the excitement must have gotten the little ones worked up too, because at that instant I felt a squeezing sensation in my lower abdomen. Like a cramp, but stronger. I shot a hand to my stomach and winced.

"What's the matter?" Tork was immediately at my side. "Is it the baby?"

The cheers and celebration of the crowd faded away as my stomach cramped again. "Yeah, I think its the baby."

"Now?" His eyes widened like saucers. "You sure?"

"Yes, now!" I snapped with a little more venom than I'd intended. A rush of wetness seeped through my pants and I winced again.

My water's broke, I thought hazily. *It's coming. The babies are actually coming.*

"Stay right here," Tork grabbed my shoulders and looked into my eyes. "It's gonna be okay. I'll get the doctor. He's gotta be here somewhere."

"You stay with your mate," Adrian interrupted us. He

must have noticed my predicament. "I'll get Dr. Parley."

"If you can find him in this mess," I moaned, looking around at the crowds of people. It would be like finding a needle in a haystack.

"I'll find him," Adrian promised and gave my hand a squeeze. "Just stay calm. I'll be right back."

With that he rushed off, pushing through the crowds of people.

Tork brushed hair away from my face and held me close. "How do you feel?"

I shifted in my seat, still cradling my stomach. "Hurts. Feels like the twins are ready to say hello. Guess they wanted to be part of the party, too."

Tork huffed. "Glad you can have some good humor about this. But what timing, huh?"

"Yeah," I chuckled. "We knew it was coming, just..."

"It's still a week away," Tork pointed out. "Your due date."

"The twins don't seem to care about due dates." I shot him a grin but it was cut off by another contraction.

"Breathe," he whispered in my ear as he rubbed my back. "Remember what I taught you. Breathe."

He was right. I let everything else fall away. The sounds of the other people around us, the music, the clink of plates and glasses. I held Tork's gaze and squeezed his hands. He kept me grounded, kept me from flying away.

"You're going to be all right," he promised. "The doctor's on his way."

And indeed he was. Adrian had located him in record time and when the doctor saw me sitting on the bench and panting for breath, he leapt into action.

"You his mate?" He eyed Tork.

"I am," Tork said. "How can I help?"

"We've got to get him out of here, back to the medical ward. The sooner the better. I've sent word to Anna to set things up and I need to go change, but you bring him right there, you hear me?"

"I will," Tork promised. "I will."

"Good. See you soon." He rushed off as soon as he'd come, and another contraction hit me like waves on the shore. I moaned and looked up at Tork through blurry eyes.

"You heard the good doctor," Tork said. "Let's get you out of here." He hooked his arms under my shoulders and knees and lifted me into the air, carrying me easily toward the door.

I knew people were staring. I knew everyone would be talking about this for weeks. But that didn't matter right now.

Tork pushed through the crowd like a steamroller, and I was once again grateful for his large stature. "Pregnant mate coming through, make way!"

People scattered in all directions and at some point I must have blacked out, because when I opened them again, we were in the medical ward.

16

TORK

We were having a baby.

No.

We were having two babies.

I couldn't believe it.

After watching Ansel grow into a man, after teaching him, mentoring him, and finally mating him, here it was. The ultimate moment. Ansel's grip just about crushed my fingers, but I let him squeeze. It was all I could do for him right now.

Doctor Parley and his nurse Anna had prepared a room for us in short order. Ansel lay on a cot with a blanket over his lower half while the doctor checked his vitals.

"Good thing you found when you did," he said,

snapping on a pair of gloves. "These little dragons are ready to meet their daddies."

Ansel gave a weak smile and I squeezed his hand again. *Remember to breathe*, I told him on our Link.

Of course I know how to breathe, you asshole. I've got babies coming out of me, that's the problem!

The sudden outburst caught me off guard and I stifled a laugh. Ansel's eyes were like daggers boring into my flesh.

So he was a little feisty while in labor. Got it.

"I'm gonna need you to push," the doctor said to Ansel. "In three...two...one..."

"Push!"

Ansel moaned in pain, his whole body tense. He squeezed my hand so tightly I lost feeling and he kept squeezing, kept yelling, kept flinging curses at me over our Link.

It will be over soon, I tried to assure him telepathically, but he wasn't having any of it.

"Almost there, I can see the head!" The doctor announced. "Push!"

Beads of sweat broke out over Ansel's forehead as he tensed and released, groaning and screaming and gritting his teeth. Whoever said omegas were weak clearly hadn't seen one giving birth. It was nothing short of miraculous.

A gasping cry of new life rent through the air and in that instant my world stopped. Nurse Anna swiftly took the baby away to clean them up, but we weren't done yet.

"One more good push for me," the doctor prodded. "I know you're tired. The little one's on the way. Now push!"

One last gasping, crying, shaking moment later, another cry joined their sibling's.

I looked to Ansel to see how he was doing. His eyes were half-lidded, his face red and covered with sweat. But in those eyes, laced with exhaustion and pain, I saw something else. Triumph. Joy. Hope.

"We did it," he muttered, finally loosening his hold on my hand. I stretched the sore fingers. "We really did it."

He closed his eyes for a moment, resting against the pillows as his breaths returned to normal.

The nurse returned with not one but two little babies in her arms, each wrapped in a swaddling newborn blanket. "Congratulations. Your little dragons are healthy and beautiful. One girl, one boy."

I let out a breath as I watched her place them into Ansel's

waiting arms. I'd never seen anything so perfect in my life. Chills ran down my spine and my dragon woke up, taking notice of the two new souls flickering to life on our Link. One girl, one boy. Ten fingers, ten toes. We'd done it.

Ansel stared at them like they were the greatest treasure on Earth. And in this moment, they were. His mouth opened and closed as he tried to find his words. Those beautiful amber eyes brimmed with tears.

"One boy, one girl," I caught Ansel's eye when he finally tore his gaze away from the twins. "What shall we call them?"

"Hmm..." Ansel thought. "You pick one, I'll pick the other?"

I shrugged. "Works for me."

"Just nothing crazy like Shadowbane or Mistwalker."

I raised an eyebrow at him. "Would I do that?"

"Knowing you? You would." He chuckled to himself.

I rolled my eyes. "Fiiine."

"Now, serious names. What do you think?"

I looked at the little girl now resting sleepily in her fathers arms. She had almost a full head of hair, unusual for a newborn. She took after her father, then. "Juno." The word came out of my mouth before I'd even realized I'd said it. The impulse came from deep within, like I somehow knew what this child would be called.

"Juno," Ansel repeated, brushing a lock of hair from the little girl's face. "I love it."

"And for the boy?" I asked.

He was a little larger, with my nose and Ansel's eyes. While his sister had calmed down and was resting on Ansel's chest, he was still screeching bloody murder. He was going to be a handful and a half, I knew.

"Ray," Ansel said and looked at me. "What do you think of Ray?"

Ray and Juno. Our twins.

"I love it," I said, and this time my voice broke with emotion. "And I love you, *nyota*," I said, slipping into the old tongue.

"Nyota?" Ansel muttered sleepily.

"My star. My shining star." I spoke reverently, to both my mate and my children. "No matter where I am, or what happens to us, you'll always be my guiding light. I'll always find my way back to you."

I love you too, Ansel said to me, only this time in my mind. I felt it latch on and take hold, deep in my soul.

I'd gone on a lot of adventures in my life. But this, right here? My mate, my two smiling babies, my family?

This was the greatest adventure of all time.

AUTHOR'S NOTE

Thank you so much for picking up this book! I hope you've come to enjoy the world and the characters of Darkvale just as much as I have.

This trilogy draws to a close, but you haven't seen the last of Darkvale! Let me know what characters you'd love to hear from next :)

If you have a moment, consider leaving a review on Amazon. It helps more people find books they love.

I've got a new series coming out soon co-written with Crista Crown. It's got more fantasy, more mpreg, and WOLVES! Keep an eye out for it soon!

May all your fires burn bright,

— Connor Crowe

When the kids are away, the mates will play...

Sign up here for your FREE copy of ONE KNOTTY NIGHT, a special story that's too hot for Amazon!

https://dl.bookfunnel.com/c1d8qcu6h8

Facebook:

fb.me/connorcrowempreg

ALSO BY CONNOR CROWE

Darkvale Dragons Series

The Dragon's Runaway Omega

The Dragon's Second-Chance Omega

The Dragon's Forbidden Omega

Darkvale Dragons Short Stories

One Knotty Night (Alec/Lucien)

Made in the USA
San Bernardino, CA
15 February 2019